I0620266

Table of Contents

FRIDAY, THE THIRTEENTH

Thomas William Lawson

 Stark Publishing

THOMAS WILLIAM LAWSON

Book Layout © 2014 BookDesignTemplates.com

Cover Design: Stark Publishing – Original Stock Image "Scary date of Friday 13th" Licensed from Getty Images

Friday, the Thirteenth – Introduced by Mark Leslie

Thomas William Lawson

FRIDAY, THE THIRTEENTH

For those who deal with paraskevidekatriaphobia

Introduction by Mark Leslie

IN MY ONGOING writing about the paranormal, I was doing research on Friday the 13th. Among my readings, I encountered a good number of intriguing facts about that well-known unlucky date which will be included in a special post-text section of this book for your enjoyment.

But, among the interesting things I discovered was this 1907 novel written by Thomas W. Lawson.

THOMAS WILLIAM LAWSON

Born on February 26, 1857 in Charleston, Massachusetts, Lawson was an American businessman and an author. As a stock broker, Lawson was highly controversial, known for his efforts to promote reforms in the stock markets as well as for manipulating those markets in order to amass a large fortune.

Lawson was, allegedly, a highly superstitious man and selected an unlucky Friday, the 13th, for the setting of this novel.

The novel sold more than 60,000 copies in its first month and even went on to be produced as a feature-length silent film. According to a 1925 New York Times article, after the novel's release, stock brokers adopted the habit of being unlikely to buy or sell stocks on this unlucky day.

In keeping with Lawson's superstitious beliefs, a terrible fate occurred to a ship that had been created in his honor.

An old saying associated with Friday the 13th is that if you leave the calendar on Friday the 13th, the devil will get you on the 14th.

That is apparently what happened to this particular ship.

The ship, the *Thomas W. Lawson* was a seven-masted, steel-hulled schooner. It was primarily used for hauling coal and oil along the East Coast of the United States. The ship was initially launched in 1902 held the distinction of being the largest schooner and sailing vessel ever built without an auxiliary engine.

Thomas W. Lawson was destroyed off the uninhabited island of Annet, in the Isles of Scilly, in a storm on Saturday December 14, 1907, killing all but two of her eighteen crew. Captain George W. Dow and engineer Edward L. Rowe from Boston were the only survivors.

FRIDAY, THE THIRTEENTH

The ship's cargo of 58,000 barrels of paraffin oil caused what is considered the first massive marine oil spill.

Large pieces of the shattered and broken wreck were relocated in 1969 some four hundred meters away from one another, the bow resting a mere 56 feet deep near Shag Rock. Under the proper weather conditions, scuba divers can visit it. A recovered anchor from the vessel was built into the outside wall of Bleak House, Broadstairs, the former home of Charles Dickens.

FRIDAY, THE THIRTEENTH

A NOVEL BY

THOMAS W. LAWSON

FRIDAY, THE THIRTEENTH

To Her

I Dedicate This Book

All That Is Good In This Little Waif, Which Is Very

Dear To Me, I Know A Just God Will Place To

Her Credit. All That Is Mean And Low And

Human Could Never Have Been Birthed

Had She Been Nigh To Guide An

Ever Wayward Pen.

The Author.

The Nest, Dreamwold,

August, 1906.

Chapter I

"FRIDAY, THE 13TH; I thought as much. If Bob has started, there will be hell, but I will see what I can do."

The sound of my voice, as I dropped the receiver, seemed to part the mists of five years and usher me into the world of Then as though it had never passed on.

I had been sitting in my office, letting the tape slide through my fingers while its every yard spelled "panic" in a constantly rising voice, when they told me that Brownley on the floor of the Exchange wanted me at the 'phone, and "quick." Brownley was our junior partner and floor man. He talked with a rush. Stock Exchange floor men in panics never let their speech hobble.

"Mr. Randolph, it's sizzling over here, and it's getting hotter every second. It's Bob—that is evident to all. If he keeps up this pace for twenty minutes longer, the sulphur will overflow 'the Street' and get into the banks and into the country, and no man can tell how much territory will be burned over by to-morrow. The boys have begged me to ask you to throw yourself into the breach and stay him. They agree you are the only hope now."

"Are you sure, Fred, that this is Bob's work?" I asked. "Have you seen him?"

"Yes, I have just come from his office, and glad I was to get out. He's on the war-path, Mr. Randolph—uglier than I ever saw him. The last time he broke loose was child's play to his mood to-day. Mother sent me word this morning that she saw last night the spell was coming. He had been up to see her and sisters, and mother thought from his tone he was about to disappear again. When she told me of his mood, and I remembered the day, I was afraid he might seek his vent here. Also

I heard of his being about town till long after midnight. The minute I opened his office door this morning he flew at me like a panther. I told him I had only dropped in on my rounds for an order, as they were running off right smart, and I didn't know but he might like to pick up some bargains. 'Bargains!' he roared, 'don't you know the day? Don't you know it is Friday, the 13th? Go back to that hell-pit and sell, sell, sell.' 'Sell what and how much?' I asked. 'Anything, everything. Give the thieves every share they will take, and when they won't take any more, ram as much again down their crops until they spit up all they have been buying for the last three months!' Going out I met Jim Holliday and Frank Swan rushing in. They are evidently executing Bob's orders, and have been pouring Anti-People's out for an hour. They will be on the floor again in a few minutes, so I thought it safer to call you before I started to sell. Mr. Randolph, they cannot take much more of anything in here, and if I begin to throw stocks over, it will bring the gavel inside of ten minutes; and that will be to announce a dozen failures. It's yet twenty minutes to one and God only knows what will happen before three. It's up to you, Mr. Randolph, to do something, and unless I am on a bad slant, you haven't many minutes to lose."

It was then I dropped the receiver with "I thought as much!" As I had been fingering the tape, watching five and ten millions crumbling from price values every few minutes, I was sure this was the work of Bob Brownley. No one else in Wall Street had the power, the nerve, and the devilish cruelty to rip things as they had been ripped during the last twenty minutes. The night before I had passed Bob in the theatre lobby. I gave him close scrutiny and saw the look of which I of all men best knew the meaning. The big brown eyes were set on space; the outer corners of the handsome mouth were drawn hard and tense as though weighted. As I had my wife with me it was impossible to follow him, but when I got home I called up his house and his clubs, intending to ask, him to run up and smoke a cigar with me, but could locate him nowhere. I tried again in the morning without success, but when just before noon the tape began to jump and flash and snarl, I remembered Bob's ugly mood, and all it portended.

Fred Brownley was Bob's youngest brother, twelve years his junior. He had been with Randolph & Randolph from the day he left college, and for over a year had been our most trusted Stock Exchange man. Bob Brownley, when himself, was as fond of his "baby brother," as he called him, as his beautiful Southern mother was of both; but when the devil had possession of Bob—and his option during the past five years had been exercised many a time—mother and brother had to take their place with all the rest of the world, for then Bob knew no kindred, no friends. All the wide world was to him during those periods a jungle peopled with savage animals and reptiles to hunt and fight and tear and kill.

It is hardly necessary for me to explain who Randolph & Randolph are. For more than sixty years the name has spoken for itself in every part of the world where dollar-making machines are installed. No railroad is financed, no great "industrial" projected, without by force of habit, hat-in-handing a by-your-leave of Randolph & Randolph, and every nation when entering the market for loans, knows that the favour of the foremost American bankers is something which must be reckoned with. I pride myself that at forty-two, at the end of the ten years I have had the helm of Randolph & Randolph, I have done nothing to mar the great name my father and uncle created, but something to add to its sterling reputation for honest dealing, fearless, old-fashioned methods, and all-round integrity. Bradstreet's and other mercantile agencies say, in reporting Randolph & Randolph, "Worth fifty millions and upward, credit unlimited." I can take but small praise for this, for the report was about the same the day I left college and came to the office to "learn the business." But, as the survivor of my great father and uncle, I can say, my Maker as my witness, that Randolph & Randolph have never loaned a dollar of their millions at over legal rates, 6 per cent, per annum; have never added to their hoard by any but fair, square business methods; and that blight of blights, frenzied finance, has yet to find a lodging-place beneath the old black-and-gold sign that father and uncle nailed up with their own hands over the entrance.

Nineteen years ago I was graduated from Harvard. My classmate and chum, Bob Brownley, of Richmond, Va., was graduated with me. He was class poet, I, yard marshal. We had been four years together at St. Paul's previous to entering Harvard. No girl and lover were fonder than we of each other.

My people had money, and to spare, and with it a hard-headed, Northern horse-sense. The Brownleys were poor as church mice, but they had the brilliant, virile blood of the old Southern oligarchy and the romantic, "salaam-to-no-one" Dixie-land pride of before-the-war days, when Southern prodigality and hospitality were found wherever women were fair and men's mirrors in the bottom of their julep-glasses.

Bob's father, one of the big, white pillars of Southern aristocracy, had gone through Congress and the Senate of his country to the tune of "Spend and not spare," which left his widow and three younger daughters and a small son dependent upon Bob, his eldest.

Many a warm summer's afternoon, as Bob and I paddled down the Charles, and often on a cold, crispy night as we sat in my shooting-box on the Cape Cod shore, had we matched up for our future. I was to have the inside run of the great banking business of Randolph & Randolph, and Bob was eventually to represent my father's firm on the floor of the Stock Exchange. "I'd die in an office," Bob used to say, "and the floor of the Stock Exchange is just the chimney-place to roast my hoe-cake in." So when our college days were over my able had saddled Bob's youth with the heavy responsibilities of husbanding and directing his family's slim finances that he took to business as a swallow to the air. We entered the office of Randolph & Randolph on the same day, and on its anniversary, a year later, my father summoned us into his office for a sort of tally-up talk. Neither of us quite knew what was coming, and we thrilled with pleasure when he said:

"Jim, you and Bob have fairly outdone my expectations. I have had my eye on both of you and I want you to know that the kind of industry and business intelligence you have shown here would have won you recognition in any banking-house on 'the Street.' I want you both in the firm—Jim to learn his way round so he can step into my shoes; you, Bob, to take one of the firm's seats on the Stock Exchange."

Bob's face went red and then pale with happiness as he reached for my father's hand.

"I'm very grateful to you sir, far more so than any words can say, but I want to talk this proposition of yours over with Jim here first. He knows me better than any one else in the world and I've some ideas I'd like to thrash out with him."

"Speak up here, Bob," said my father.

"Well, sir, I should feel much better if I could go over there into the swirl and smash it out for myself. You see if I could win out alone and pay back the seat price, and then make a pile for myself, if you felt later like giving me another chance to come into the firm, then I should not be laying myself open to the charge of being a mere pensioner on your friendship. You know what I mean, sir, and won't think I am filled with any low-down pride, but if you will let me have the price of a Stock Exchange seat on my note, and will give me the chance, when I get the hang of the ropes, to handle some of the firm's orders, I shall be just as much beholden to you and Jim, sir, and shall feel a lot better myself."

I knew what Bob meant; so did father, and we were glad enough to do what he asked, father insisting on making the seat price in the form of a present, after explaining to us that a foundation Stock Exchange rule prohibited an applicant from borrowing the seat price. Four years after Bob Brownley entered the Stock Exchange he had paid back the forty thousand, with interest, and not only had a snug fifty thousand to his credit on Randolph & Randolph's books, but was sending home six thousand a year while living up to, as he jokingly put it, "an honest man's notch." I may say in passing, that a Wall Street man's notch would make twice six thousand yearly earnings cast an uncertain shadow at Christmas time. Bob was the favourite of the Exchange, as he had been the pet at school and at college, and had his hands full of business three hundred days in the year. Besides Randolph & Randolph's choicest commissions, he had the confidential orders of two of the heavy plunging cliques.

I had just passed my thirty-second birthday when my kind old dad suddenly died. For the previous six years I had been getting ready for such an event; that is, I had grown accustomed to hearing my father say: "Jim, don't let any grass grow in getting the hang of every branch of our business, so that when anything happens to me there will be no disturbance in 'the Street' in regard to Randolph & Randolph's affairs. I want to let the world know as soon as possible that after I am gone our business will run as it always has. So I will work you into my directorships in those companies where we have interests and gradually put you into my different trusteeships."

Thus at father's death there was not a ripple in our affairs and none of the stocks known as "The Randolph's" fluttered a point because of that, to the financial world, momentous event. I inherited all of father's fortune other than four millions, which he divided up among relatives and charities, and took command of a business that gave me an income of two millions and a half a year.

Once more I begged Bob to come into the firm.

"Not yet, Jim," he replied. "I've got my seat and about a hundred thousand capital, and I want to feel that I'm free to kick my heels until I have raked together an even million all of my own making; then I'll settle down with you, old man, and hold my handle of the plough, and if some good girl happens along about that time—well, then it will be 'An ivy-covered little cot' for mine."

He laughed, and I laughed too. Bob was looked upon by all his friends as a bad case of woman-shy. No woman, young or old, who had in any way crossed Bob's orbit but had felt that fascination, delicious to all women, in the presence of:

A soul by honour schooled,

A heart by passion ruled—

but he never seemed to see it. As my wife—for I had been three years married and had two little Randolphs to show that both Katherine Blair and I knew what marriage was for—never tired of saying, "Poor Bob! He's woman-blind, and it looks as though he would never get his sight in that direction."

"Then again, Jim," he continued in a tone of great seriousness, "there's a little secret I have never let even you into. The truth is I am not safe yet—not safe to speak for the old house of Randolph & Randolph. Yes, you may laugh—you who are, and always have been, as staunch and steady as the old bronze John Harvard in the yard, you who know Monday mornings just what you are going to do Saturday nights and all the days and nights in between, and who always do it. Jim, I have found since I have been over on the floor that the Southern gambling blood that made my grandfather, on one of his trips back from New York, though he had more land and slaves than he could use, stake his land and slaves—yes, and grandmother's too—on a card-game, and—lose, and change the whole face of the Brownley destiny—those same gambling microbes are in my blood, and when they begin to claw and gnaw I want to do something; and, Jim"—and the big brown eyes suddenly shot sparks—"if those microbes ever get unleashed, there'll be mischief to pay on the floor—sure there will!"

Bob's handsome head was thrown back; his thin nostrils dilated as though there was in them the breath of conflict. The lips were drawn across the white teeth with just part enough to show their edges, and in the depths of the eyes was a dark-red blaze that somehow gave the impression one gets in looking down some long avenue of black at the instant a locomotive headlight rounds a curve at night.

Twice before, way back in our college days, I had had a peep at this gambling tempter of Bob's. Once in a poker game in our rooms, when a crowd of New York classmates tried to run him out of a hand by the sheer weight of coin. And again at the Pequot House at New London on the eve of a varsity boat-race, when a Yale crowd shook a big wad of money and taunts at Bob until with a yell he left his usually well-leaded feet and frightened me, whose allowance was dollars to Bob's cents, at the sum total of the bet-cards he signed before he cleared the room of Yale money and came to with a white face streaming with cold perspiration. These events had passed out of my memory as the ordinary student breaks that any hot-blooded youth is liable to make in like circumstances. As I looked at Bob that day, while he tried to tell me that the business of Randolph & Randolph would not be safe in his keeping, I had to admit to myself that I was puzzled. I had regarded my old college chum not only as the best mentally harnessed man I had ever met, but I knew him as the soul of honour, that honour of the old story-books, and I could not credit his being tempted to jeopardise unfairly the rights or property of another. But it was habit with me to let Bob have his way, and I did not press him to come into our firm as a full partner.

FRIDAY, THE THIRTEENTH

Five years later, during which time affairs, business and social, had been slipping along as well as either Bob or I could have asked, I was preparing for another sit-down to show my chum that the time had now come for him to help me in earnest, when a queer thing happened—one of those unaccountable incidents that God sometimes sees fit to drop across the life-paths of His children, paths heretofore as straight and far-ahead-visible as highways along which one has never to look twice to see where he is travelling; one of those events that, looked at retrospectively, are beyond all human understanding.

It was a beautiful July Saturday noon and Bob and I had just "packed up" for the day preparatory to joining Mrs. Randolph on my yacht for a run down to our place at Newport. As we stepped out of his office one of the clerks announced that a lady had come in and had particularly asked to see Mr. Brownley.

"Who the deuce can she be, coming in at this time on Saturday, just when all alive men are in a rush to shake the heat and dirt of business for food and the good air of all outdoors?" growled Bob. Then he said, "Show her in."

Another minute and he had his answer.

A lady entered.

"Mr. Brownley?" She waited an instant to make sure he was the Virginian.

Bob bowed.

"I am Beulah Sands, of Sands Landing, Virginia. Your people know our people, Mr. Brownley, probably well enough for you to place me."

"Of the Judge Lee Sands's?" asked Bob, as he held out his hand.

"I am Judge Lee Sands's oldest daughter," said the sweetest voice I had ever heard, one of those mellow, rippling voices that start the imagination on a chase for a mocking-bird, only to bring it up at the pool beneath the brook-fall in quest of the harp of moss and watercresses that sends a bubbling cadence into its eddies and swirls. Perhaps it was the Southern accent that nibbled off the corners and edges of certain words and languidly let others mist themselves together, that gave it its luscious penetration—however that may be, it was the most no-yesterday-no-tomorrow voice I had ever heard. Before I grew fully conscious of the exquisite beauty of the girl, this voice of hers spelled its way into my brain like the breath of some bewitching Oriental essence. Nature, environment, the security of a perfect marriage have ever combined to constitute me loyal to my chosen one, yet as I stood silent, like one dumb, absorbing the details of the loveliness of this young stranger who had so suddenly swept into my office, it came over me that here was a woman intended to enlighten men who could not understand that shaft which in all ages has without warning pierced men's hearts and souls—love at first sight. Had there not been Katherine Blair, wife and mother—Katherine Blair Randolph, who filled my love-world as the noonday August sun fills the old-fashioned well with nestling warmth and restful shade—after this interval, looking back at the past, I dare ask the question—who knows but that I too might have drifted from the secure anchorage of my slow Yankee blood and floated into the deep waters?

Beauty, the cynic's scoff, is in the eye of the beholder, or in an angle of vision—mere product of lime-light, point of view, desire—but Beulah Sands's was beauty beyond cavil, superior to all analysis, as definite as the evening star against the twilight sky. In height medium, girlish, but with a figure maturely modelled, charmingly full and rounded, yet by very perfection of proportion escaping suggestion of "plumpness." The head, surrounded and crowned with a wealth of dark golden hair, rested on a neck that would have seemed short had its slender column sprung less graciously from the lovely lines of the breast and shoulders beneath. It was on the face, however, and finally on the eyes that one's glances inevitably lingered—the face rose-tinted, with dimples in either of the full cheeks, entering laughing protest against the sad droop that brought slightly down the corners of a mouth too large perhaps for beauty, if the coral curve of the lips had been less exquisitely perfect. The straight, thin-nostriled nose, the broad forehead, the square, full jaw almost as low at the points where they come beneath the ears as at the chin, suggested dignity and high resolve coupled with a power of purpose, rare in woman. The combination of forehead, jaw, and nose was seldom seen. Had it been possessed by a man it would surely have driven him to the tented field for his profession. But the greatest glory of Beulah Sands was her eyes—large, full, very gray, very blue, vivid with all the glamour of her personality, full of smiles and tears and spirituality and passion; one instant, frankly innocent, they illuminated the face of a blonde Madonna; the next, seen through the extraordinary, long, jet-black eye-lashes underneath the finely pencilled black brows, they caressed, coquetted, allured. I afterward found much of this girl's purely physical fascination lay in this strange blending of English fairness with Andalusian tints, though the abiding quality of her charm was surely in an exaltation of spirit of which she might make the dullest conscious. As she stood looking at Bob in my office that long-ago noon, gracefully at ease in a suit of gray, with a gray-feathered turban on her head, and tiny lace bands at neck and wrist, she was very exquisite, exceedingly dainty, and, though Southerner of Southerners, very unlike the typical brunette girl who comes out of Dixie land.

This girl who came into our office that July Saturday, just in time to interfere with the outing Bob Brownley and I had laid out, and who was destined to divert my chum's heretofore smooth-flowing river of existence and turn it into an alternation of roaring rushes and deadly calms, was truly the most exquisite creature one could conceive of, I know my thought must have been Bob's too, for his eyes were riveted on her face. She dropped the black lashes like a veil as she went on:

"Mr. Brownley, I have just come from Sands Landing. I am very anxious to talk with you on a business matter. I have brought a letter to you from my father. If you have other engagements I can wait until Monday, although," and the black veiling lashes lifted, showing the half-laughing, half-pathetic eyes, "I wanted much to lay my business before you at the earliest minute possible."

There was a faint touch of appeal in the charming voice as she spoke that was irresistible, and we were both willing to forget we had lunch waiting us on the *Tribesman*.

"Step into my office, Miss Sands, and all my time is yours," said Bob, as he opened the door between his office and mine. After I had sent a note to my wife, saying we might be delayed for an hour or two, I settled down to wait for Bob in the general office, and it was a long wait. Thirty minutes went into an hour and an hour into two before Bob and Miss Sands came out. After he had put her in a cab for her hotel, he said in a tone curiously intent: "Jim, I have got to talk with you, got to get some of your good advice. Suppose we hustle along to the yacht and after lunch you tell Kate we have some business to go over. I don't want to keep that girl waiting any longer than possible for an answer I cannot give until I get your ideas." After lunch, on the bow end of the upper deck Bob relieved himself. Relieved is the word, for from the minute he had put Miss Sands into the carriage until then, it was evident even to my wife that his thoughts were anywhere but upon our outing.

"Jim," he began in a voice that shook in spite of his efforts to make it sound calm, "there is no disguising the fact that I am mightily worked up about this matter, and I want to do everything possible for this girl. No need of my telling you how sacred we have got to keep what she has just let me into. You'll see as I go along that it is sacred, and I know you will look at it as I do. Miss Sands must be helped out of her trouble.

"Judge Lee Sands, her father, is the head of the old Sands family of Virginia. The Virginia Sands don't take off their bonnets to another family in this country, or elsewhere, for that matter, for anything that really counts. They have had brains, learning, money, and fixed position since Virginia was first settled. They are the best people of our State. It is a cross-road saying in Virginia that a Sands of Sands Landing can go to the bench, the United States Senate, the House, or the governor's chair for the starting, and nearly all of the men folks have held one or all of these honours for generations. The present judge has held them all. I don't know him personally, although my people and his have been thick from away back. Sands Landing on the James is some fifty miles above our home. The judge, Beulah Sands's father, is close on to seventy, and I have heard mother and father say is a stalwart, a Virginia stalwart. Being rich—that is, what we Virginians call rich, a million or so—he has been very active in affairs, and I knew before his daughter told me, that he was the trustee for about all the best estates in our part of the country. It seems from what she tells, that of late he has been very active in developing our coal-mines and railroads, and that particularly he took a prominent hand in the Seaboard Air Line. You know the road, for your father was a director, and I think the house has been prominent in its banking affairs. Now, Jim, this poor girl, who, it seems, has recently been acting as the judge's secretary, has just learned that that coup of Reinhart and his crowd has completely ruined her father. The decline has swamped his own fortune, and, what is worse, a million to a million and a half of his trust funds as well, and the old judge—well, you and I can understand his position. Yet I do not know that you just can, either, for you do not quite understand our Virginia life and the kind of revered position a man like Judge Sands occupies. You would have to know that to understand fully his present purgatory and the terrible position of this daughter, for it seems that since he began to get into deep water he has been relying upon her for courage and ideas. From our talk I gather she has a wonderful store of up-to-date business notions, and I am convinced from what she lays out that the judge's affairs are hopeless, and, Jim, when that old man goes down it will be a smash that will shake our State in more ways than one.

"Up to now the girl has stood up to the blow like a man and has been able to steady the judge until he presents an exterior that holds down suspicion as to his real financial condition, although she says Reinhart and his Baltimore lawyer, from the ruthless way they put on the screws to shake out his holdings in the Air Line, must have a line on it that the judge is overboard. The old gentleman can keep things going for six months longer without jeopardising any of the remaining trust funds, of which he has some two millions, and while his wife, who is an invalid, knows the judge is in some trouble, she does not suspect his real position. His daughter says that when the blow came, that day of the panic, when Reinhart jammed the stock out of sight and scuttled her father's bankers and partners in the road, the Wilsons of Baltimore, she had a frightful struggle to keep her father from going insane. She told me that for three days and nights she kept him locked in their rooms at their hotel in Baltimore, to prevent him from hunting Reinhart and his lawyer Rettybone and killing them both, but that at last she got him calmed down and together they have been planning.

"Jim, it was tough to sit there and listen to the schemes to recoup that this old gentleman and this girl, for she is only twenty-one, have tried to hatch up. The tears actually rolled down my cheeks as I listened; I couldn't help it; you couldn't either, Jim. But at last out of all the plans considered, they found only one that had a tint of hope in it, and the serious mention of even that one, Jim, in any but present circumstances, would make you think we were dealing with lunatics. But the girl has succeeded in making me think it worth trying. Yes, Jim, she has, and I have told her so, and I hope to God that that hard-headed horse-sense of yours will not make you sit down on it."

Bob Brownley had got to his feet; he was slipping the shackles of that fiery, romantic, Southern passion that years in college and Wall Street had taught him to keep prisoner. His eyes were flashing sparks. His nostrils vibrated like a deer buck's in the autumn woods. He faced me with his hands clinched.

"Jim Randolph," he went on, "as I listened to that girl's story of the terrible cruelty and devilish treachery practised by the human hyenas you and I associate with, human hyenas who, when in search of dirty dollars—the only thing they know anything about—put to shame the real beasts of the wilds—when I listened, I tell you that I felt it would not give me a twinge of conscience to put a ball through that slick scoundrel Reinhart. Yes, and that hired cur of his, too, who prostitutes a good family name and position, and an inherited ability the Almighty intended for more honest uses than the trapping of victims on whose purses his gutter-born master has set lecherous eyes. And, Jim, as I listened, a troop of old friends invaded my memory—friends whom I have not seen since before I went to Harvard, friends with whom I spent many a happy hour in my old Virginia home, friends born of my imagination, stalwart, rugged crusaders, who carried the sword and the cross and the banner inscribed 'For Honour and for God.' Old friends who would troop into my boyhood and trumpet, 'Bob, don't forget, when you're a man, that the goal is honour, and the code: Do unto your neighbour as you would have your neighbour do unto you. Don't forget that millions is the crest of the groundlings.' And, Jim, I thought my friends looked at me with reproachful eyes, as they said, 'You are well on the road, Bob Brownley, and in time your heart and soul will bear the hall-mark of the snaky S on the two upright bars, and you will be but a frenzied fellow in the Dirty Dollar army.' Jim, Jim Randolph, as I listened to that agonising tale of the changing of that girl's heaven to hell, I did not see that halo you and I have thought surrounded the sign of Randolph & Randolph. I did not see it, Jim, but I did see myself, and I didn't feel proud of the picture. My God, Jim, is it possible you and I have joined the nobility of Dirty Dollars? Is it possible we are leaving trails along our life's path like that Reinhart left through the home of these Virginians, such trails as this girl has shown me?"

Bob had worked himself into a state of frenzy. I had never seen him so excited as when he stood in front of me and almost shouted this fierce self-denunciation.

"For heaven's sake, Bob, pull yourself together," I urged. "The captain on the bridge there is staring at you wild-eyed, and Katherine will be up here to see what has happened. Now, be a good fellow, and let us talk this thing over in a sensible way. At the gait you are going we can do nothing to help out your friends. Besides, what is there for you and me to take ourselves to task for? We are no wreckers and none of our dollars is stained with Frenzied Finance. My father, as you know, despised Reinhart and his sort as much as we do. Be yourself. What does this girl want you to do? If it is anything in reason, call it done, for you know there is nothing I won't do for you at the asking."

Bob's hysteria oozed. He dropped on the rail-seat at my side.

"I know it, Jim, I know it, and you must forgive me. The fact, is, Beulah Sands's story has aroused a lot of thoughts I have been a-sticking down cellar late years, for, to tell the truth, I have some nasty twinges of conscience every now and then when I get to thinking of this dollar game of ours."

I saw that the impulsive blood was fast cooling, and that it would only be a question of minutes until Bob would be his clearheaded self.

"Now, what is it she wants you to do?" I persisted. "Is it a case of money, of our trying to tide her father over?"

"Nothing of that kind, Jim. You don't know the proud Virginia blood. Neither that girl nor her father would accept money help from any one. They would go to smash and the grave first."

He paused and then continued impressively:

"This is how she puts it. She and her father have raked together her different legacies and turned them into cash, a matter of sixty thousand dollars, and she got him to consent to let her come up here to see if during the next six months she might not, in a few desperate plunges in the market, run it up to enough to at least regain the trust funds. Yes, I know it is a wild idea. I told her so at the beginning, but there was no need; she knew it, for she is not only bright, but she has the best idea of business I ever knew a woman to have. But it is their only chance, Jim, and while I listened to her argument I came around to her way of thinking."

"But how did she happen to come to you with this extraordinary scheme?" I interrupted.

"It's this way—her father, who knew Randolph & Randolph through your father's handling of the Seaboard's affairs, learned of my connection with the house, and gave her a letter, asking me to do what I could to help his daughter carry out her plans. She wants to get a position with us, if possible, in some sort of capacity, secretary, confidential clerk, or, as she puts it, any sort of place that will justify her being in the office. She tells me she is good at shorthand, on the machine, or at correspondence, also that she has been a contributor to the magazines. If this can be arranged, she says she will on her own responsibility select the time and the stock, and hurl the last of the Sands fortune at the market, and, Jim, she is game. The blow seems to have turned this child into a wonderfully nervy creature, and, old man, I am beginning to have a feeling that perhaps the cards may come so she will win the judge out. You and I know where less than sixty thousand has been run up to millions more than once, and that, too, without the aid she will have, for I'll surely do all I can to help her steer this last chance into spongy places."

Bob in his enthusiasm had completely lost sight of the fact that he was indorsing a project that but a moment previously he had pronounced insane, and with a start I realised what this sudden transformation betokened. Inevitably, if the project he outlined were carried out, Bob and the beautiful Southern girl would be thrown into close association with each other, and further acquaintance could only deepen the startling influence Beulah Sands had already won over my ordinarily sane and cool-headed comrade. As I looked at my friend, burning with an ardour as unaccustomed as it was impulsive, I felt a tug at my heartstrings at thought of the sudden cross-roading of his life's highway. But I, too, was filled with the glamour of this girl's wondrous beauty, and her terrible predicament appealed to me almost as strongly as it had to Bob. So, although I knew it would be fatal to any chance of his weighing the matter by common sense, I burst out:

"Bob, I don't blame you for falling in with the girl's plans. If I were in your shoes, I should too."

Tears came to Bob's eyes as he grabbed my hand and said:

"Jim, how can I ever repay you for all the good things you have done for me—how can I!"

It was no time to give way to emotional outbursts, and while Bob was getting his grip on himself, I went on:

"Come along down to earth now, Bob; let us look at this thing squarely. You and I, with our position in the market, can do lots of things to help run that sixty thousand to higher figures, but six months is a short time and a million or two a world of money."

"She knows that," he said, "and the time is much shorter and the road to go much longer than you figure," he replied. "This girl is as high-tensioned as the E string on a Stradivarius, and she declares she will have no charity tips or unusual favours from us or any one else. But let us not talk about that now or we'll get discouraged. Let's do as she says and trust to God for the outcome. Are you willing, Jim, to take her into the office as a sort of confidential secretary? If you will, I'll take charge of her account, and together we will do all that two men can for her and her father."

Chapter II

THE FOLLOWING WEEK saw Miss Sands, of Virginia, private secretary to the head of Randolph & Randolph, established in a little office between mine and Bob's. She had not been there a day before we knew she was a worker. She spent the hours going over reports and analysing financial statements, showing a sagacity extraordinary in so young a person. She explained her knowledge of figures by the hand-work she had done for the judge, all of whose accounts she had kept. Bob and I saw that she was bent on smothering her memory in that antidote for all ills of heart and soul—work. Her office life was simplicity itself. She spoke to no one except Bob, save in connection with such business matters of the firm's as I might send her by one of the clerks to attend to. To the others in the banking-house she was just an unconventional young literary woman whose high social connections had gained her this opportunity of getting at the secrets of finance, from actual experience, for use in forthcoming novels. It had got abroad that she was the writer of great distinction who, under a *nom de plume*, had recently made quite a dent in the world's literary shell—a suggestion that I rightly guessed was one of Bob's delicate ways of smoothing out her path. I had tried in every way to make things easy for her, but it was impossible for me to draw her out in talk, and finally I gave it up. Had it not been that every time I passed her office door I was compelled by the fascination which I had first felt, and which, instead of diminishing, had increased with her reticence, to look in at the quiet figure with the downcast eyes, working away at her desk as though her life depended on never missing a second, I should not have known she was in the building. My wife, at my suggestion, had tried to induce her to visit us; in fact, after I let her into just enough of Beulah Sands's story so that she could see things on a true slant, she had decided to try to bring her to our house to live. But though the girl was sweetly gentle in her appreciation of Kate's thoughtful attentions, in her simple way she made us both feel that our efforts would be for naught, that her position must be the same as that of any other clerk in the office. We both finally left her to herself. Bob explained to me, some three weeks after she came to the office, that she received no visitors at her home, a hotel on a quiet uptown street, and that even he had never had permission to call upon her there.

But from the day she came to occupy her desk in our office, Bob was a changed man, whether for better or for worse neither Kate nor I could decide. His old bounding elasticity was gone, and with it his rollicking laugh. He was now a man where before he had been a boy, a man with a burden. Even if I had not heard Beulah Sands's story, I should have guessed that Bob was staggering under a strange load. While before, from the close of the Stock Exchange until its opening the next morning, he was, as Kate was fond of putting it, always ready to fill in for anything from chaperon to nurse, always open for any lark we planned, from a Bohemian dinner to the opera, now weeks went by without our seeing him at our house. In the office it used to be a saying that outside gong-strikes, Bob Brownley did not know he was in the stock business. Formerly every clerk knew when Bob came or went, for it was with a rush, a shout, a laugh, and a bang of doors; and on the floor of the Stock Exchange no man played so many pranks, or filled his orders with so much jolly good-nature and hilarious boisterousness. But from the day the Virginian girl crossed his path, Bob Brownley was a man who was thinking, thinking, thinking all the time. It was only with an effort that he would keep his eyes on whomever he was talking with long enough to take in what was said, and if the saying occupied much time it would be apparent to the talker that Bob was off in the clouds. All his friends and associates remarked the change, but I alone, except perhaps Kate, had any idea of the cause. I knew that two million dollars and the coming New Year were hurdling like kangaroos over Bob's mental rails and ditches, though I did not know it from anything he told me, for after that talk on the upper deck of the *Tribesman* he had shut up like a clam.

He did not exactly shun me, but showed me in many ways that he had entered into a new world, in which he desired to be alone. That Beulah Sands's plight had roused into intense activity all the latent romance of my friend's nature, did not surprise me. I foresaw from the first that Bob would fall head over heels in love with this beautiful, sorrow-laden girl, and it was soon obvious that the long-delayed shaft had planted its point in the innermost depths of his being. His was more than love; a fervid idolatry now had possession of his soul, mind, and body. Yet its outward manifestations were the opposite of what one would have looked for in this gay and optimistic Southerner. It was rather priest-like worship, a calm imperturbability that nothing seemed to distract or upset, at least in the presence of the goddess who was its object. Every morning he would pass through my office headed straight for the little room she occupied as if it were his one objective point of the day, but once he heard his own "Good morning, Miss Sands," he seemed to round to, and while in her presence was the Bob Brownley of old. He would be in and out all day on any and every pretext, always entering with an undisguised eagerness, leaving with a slow, dreamy reluctance. That he never saw her outside the office, I am sure, for she said good-night to him when he or she left for the day with the same don't-come-with-me dignity that she exhibited to all the rest of us. I had not attempted to say a word to Bob about his feeling for Beulah Sands, nor had he ever brought up the subject to me. On the contrary, he studiously avoided it.

Three months of the six had now passed, and with each day I thought I noted an increasing anxiety in Bob. He had opened a special account for Miss Sands on the books of the house in his name as agent, with a credit of sixty thousand dollars, and we both watched it with a painful tenseness of scrutiny. It had grown by uneven jerks, until the balance on October 1st was almost four hundred thousand dollars. On some of the trades Bob had consulted me, and on others, two in particular where he closed up after a few days' operations with nearly two hundred thousand dollars profit, I did not even know what the trading was based on until the stocks had been sold. Then he said:

"Jim, that little lady from Virginia can give us a big handicap and play us to a standstill at our own game. She told me to buy all the Burlington and Sugar her account would stand, and did not even ask for my opinion. In both cases I thought the operations were more the result of a wakeful night and an I-must-do-something decision than anything else, and I tackled both with a shiver; but when she told me to sell them out at a time I thought they looked like going higher and the next day they slumped, I could not help thinking about the destiny that shapes our ends."

On my part I tried to help. On one occasion, without consulting her, I put her account in on a sure thing underwriting, wherein she stood to make a profit of a quarter of a million, but when Bob told her what I had done, she insisted with great dignity that her name be withdrawn. After that neither of us dared help her to any short cuts. Bob was deeply impressed by her principles, and, commenting on them, said: "Jim, if all Wall Street had a code similar to Beulah Sands's to hew to in their gambles, ours would be a fairer and more manly game, and many of the multi-millionaires would be clerking, while a lot of the hand-to-mouth traders would come downtown in a new auto every day in the week. She does not believe in stock-gambling. She has worked it out that every dollar one man makes, another loses; that the one who makes gives nothing in return for what he gets away with; and that the other fellow's loss makes him and his as miserable as would robbery to the same amount. Yet she realises that she must get back those millions stolen from her father and is willing to smother her conscience to attempt it, provided she takes no unfair advantage of the other players.

The other day she said to me, 'I have decided, because of my duty to my father, to put away my prejudice against gambling, but no duty to him or to any one can justify me in playing with marked cards.' Jim, there is food for reflection for you and me, don't you think so?"

I did not argue it with him, for, after that Saturday's outburst, I had made up my mind to avoid stirring Bob up unnecessarily. Also, I had to admit to myself that the things he had then said had raised some uncomfortable thoughts in me, thoughts that made me glance less confidently now and then at the old sign of Randolph & Randolph and at the big ledger which showed that I, an ordinary citizen of a free country, was the absolute possessor of more money than a hundred thousand of my fellow beings together could accumulate in a lifetime, although each one had worked harder, longer, more conscientiously, and with perhaps more ability than I.

As to how Beulah Sands's code had affected my friend, I was ignorant. For the first time in our association I was completely in the dark as to what he was doing stockwise. Up to that Saturday I was the first to whom he would rush for congratulations when he struck it rich over others on the exchange, and he invariably sought me for consolation when the boys "upper-cut him hard," as he would put it. Now he never said a word about his trading. I saw that his account with the house was inactive, that his balance was about the same as before Miss Sands's advent, and I came to the conclusion that he was resting on his oars and giving his undivided attention to her account and the execution of his commissions. His handling of the business of the house showed no change. He still was the best broker on the floor. However, knowing Bob as I did, I could not get it out of my mind that his brain was running like a mill-race in search of some successful solution to the tremendous problem that must be solved in the next three months.

Shortly after the October 1st statements had been sent out, Bob dropped in on Kate and me one night. After she had retired and we had lit our cigars in the library he said:

"Jim, I want some of that old-fashioned advice of yours. Sugar is selling at 110, and it is worth it; in fact it is cheap. The stock is well distributed among investors, not much of it floating round 'the Street.' A good, big buying movement, well handled, would jump it to 175 and keep it there. Am I sound?"

I agreed with him.

"All right. Now what reason is there for a good, big, stiff uplift? That tariff bill is up at Washington. If it goes through, Sugar will be cheaper at 175 than at 110."

Again I agreed.

"'Standard Oil' and the Sugar people know whether it is going through, for they control the Senate and the House and can induce the President to be good. What do you say to that?"

"O.K.," I answered.

"No question about it, is there?"

"Not the slightest."

"Right again. When 26 Broadway[1] gives the secret order to the Washington boss and he passes it out to the grafters, there will be a quiet accumulation of the stock, won't there?"

"You've got that right, Bob."

"And the man who first knows when Washington begins to take on Sugar is the man who should load up quick and rush it up to a high

36

level. If he does it quickly, the stockholders, who now have it, will get a juicy slice of the ripening melon, a slice that otherwise would go to those greedy hypocrites at Washington, who are always publicly proclaiming that they are there to serve their fellow countrymen, but who never tire of expressing themselves to their brokers as not being in politics for their health."

"So far, good reasoning," I commented.

"Jim, the man who first knows when the Senators and Congressmen and members of the Cabinet begin to buy Sugar, is the man who can kill four birds with one stone: Win back a part of Judge Sands's stolen fortune; increase his own pile against the first of January, when, if the little Virginian lady is short a few hundred thousand of the necessary amount, he could, if he found a way to induce her to accept it, supply the deficiency; fatten up a good friend's bank account a million or so, and do a right good turn for the stockholders who are about to be, for the hundredth time, bled out of profit rightfully theirs."

Bob was afire with enthusiasm, the first I had seen him show for three months. Seeing that I had followed him without objection so far, he continued:

"Well, Jim, I know the Washington buying has begun. All I know I have dug out for myself and am free to use it any way I choose. I have gone over the deal with Beulah Sands, and we have decided to plunge. She has a balance of about four hundred thousand dollars, and I'm going to spread it thin. I am going to buy her 20,000 shares and to take on 10,000 for myself. If you went in for 20,000 more, it would give me a wide sea to sail in. I know you never speculate, Jim, for the house, but I thought you might in this case go in personally."

"Don't say anything more, Bob," I replied. "This time the rule goes by the board. But I will do better: I'll put up a million and you can go as high as 70,000 for me. That will give you a buying power of 100,000, and I want you to use my last 50,000 shares as a lifter."

I had never speculated in a share of stock since I entered the firm of Randolph & Randolph, and on general, special, and every other principle was opposed to stock gambling, but I saw how Bob had worked it out, and that to make the deal sure it was necessary for him to have a good reserve buying power to fall back on if, after he got started, the "System" masters, whose game he was butting in to and whose plans he might upset should try to shake down the price to drive him out of their preserves. Bob knew how I looked at his proposed deal and ordinarily would not have allowed me to have the short end of it, but so changed had he become in his anxiety to make that money for the Virginians that he grabbed at my acceptance.

"Thank you, Jim," he said fervently, and he continued: "Of course, I see what's going through your head, but I'll accept the favour, for the deal is bound to be successful. I know your reason for coming in is just to help out, and that you won't feel badly because your last 50,000 shares will be used more as a guarantee for the deal's success than for profit. And Miss Sands could not object to the part you play, as she did at the underwriting, for you will get a big profit anyway."

Next day Sugar was lively on the Exchange. Bob bought all in sight and handled the buying in a masterly way. When the closing gong struck, Beulah Sands had 20,000 shares, which averaged her 115; Bob and I had 30,000 at an average of 125, and the stock had closed 132 bid and in big demand. Miss Sands's 20,000 showed $340,000 profit, while our 30,000 showed $210,000 at the closing price. All the houses with Washington wires were wildly scrambling for Sugar as soon as it began to jump. And it certainly looked as though the shares were good for the figures set for them by Bob, $175, at which price the Sands's profits would be $1,200,000. Bob was beside himself with joy. He dined with

Kate and me, and as I watched him my heart almost stopped beating at the thought—"if anything should happen to upset his plans!" His happiness was pathetic to witness. He was like a child. He threw away all the reserve of the past three months and laughed and was grave by turns. After dinner, as we sat in the library over our coffee, he leaned over to my wife and said:

"Katherine Randolph, you and Jim don't know what misery I have been in for three months, and now—will to-morrow never come, so I may get into the whirl and clean up this deal and send that girl back to her father with the money! I wanted her to telegraph the judge that things looked like she would win out and bring back the relief, but she would not hear of it. She is a marvellous woman. She has not turned a hair to-day. I don't think her pulse is up an eighth to-night. She has not sent home a word of encouragement since she has been here, more than to tell her father she is doing well with her stories. It seems they both agreed that the only way to work the thing out was 'whole hog or none,' and that she was to say nothing until she could herself bring the word 'saved' or 'lost.' I don't know but she is right. She says if she should raise her father's hopes, and then be compelled to dash them, the effect would be fatal."

Bob rushed the talk along, flitting from one point to another, but invariably returning to Beulah Sands and to-morrow and its saving profits. Finally, he got to a pitch where it seemed as though he must take off the lid, and before Kate or I realised what was coming he placed himself in front of us and said:

"Jim, Kate, I cannot go into to-morrow without telling you something that neither of you suspect. I must tell some one, now that everything is coming out right and that Beulah is to be saved; and whom can I tell but you, who have been everything to me?—I love Beulah Sands, surely, deeply, with every bit of me. I worship her, I tell you, and to-morrow, to-morrow if this deal comes out as it must come, and I can put $1,500,000 into her hands and send her home to her father, then, then, I will tell her I love her, and Jim, Kate, if she'll marry me, good-bye, good-bye to this hell of dollar-hunting, good-bye to such misery as I have been in for three months, and home, a Virginia home, for Beulah and me." He sank into a chair and tears rolled down his cheeks Poor, poor Bob, strong as a lion in adversity, hysterical as a woman with victory in sight.

The next day Sugar opened with a wild rush: "25,000 shares from 140 to 152." That is the way it came on the tape, which meant that the crowd around the Sugar-pole was a mob and that the transactions were so heavy, quick, and tangled that no one could tell to a certainty just what the first or opening price was; but after the first lull, after the gong, there were officially reported transactions aggregating 25,000 shares and at prices varying from 140 to 152. I was over on the floor to see the scramble, for it was noised about long before ten o'clock that Sugar would open wild, and then, too, I wanted to be handy if Bob should need any quick advice.

A minute before the gong struck, there were three hundred men jammed around the Sugar-pole; men with set, determined faces; men with their coats buttoned tight and shoulders thrown back for the rush to which, by comparison, that of a football team is child's play. Every man in that crowd was a picked man, picked for what was coming. Each felt that upon his individual powers to keep a clear head, to shout loudest, to forget nothing, to keep his feet, and to stay as near the centre of the crowd as possible, depended his "floor honour," perhaps his fortune, or, what was more to him, his client's fortune. Nearly every man of them was a college graduate who had won his spurs at athletics or a seasoned floor man whose training had been even more severe than that of the college campus. When it is known before the opening of the Exchange that there are to be "things doing" in a certain stock, it is the rule to send only the picked floor men into the crowd. There may be a fortune to make or to lose in a minute or a sliver of a minute. For instance, the man who that morning was able to snatch the first 5,000 shares sold at 140 could have resold them a few minutes afterward at 152 and secured $60,000 profit. And the man who was sent into the crowd by his client to sell 5,000 shares at the "opening" and who got but 140, when the price would be 152 by the time he reported to his customer, was a man to be pitied. Again, the trader who the night before had decided that Sugar had gone up too fast, and who had "shorted" (that is, sold what he did not have, with the intention of repurchasing at a lower price than he sold it for) 5,000 shares at 140 and who, finding himself in that surging mob with Sugar selling at 152, could only get out by taking a loss of $60,000, or by taking another chance of later paying 162—such a trader was also to be pitied.

No one who scanned the crowd that morning would have believed that the calm, set face on that erect Indian figure, occupying the very centre of that horde of gamblers who were only awaiting the ringing clang of the gong to hurl themselves like madmen at each other, was the hysterical man who the night before was wildly praying for this moment. Nearly every man in that crowd was calm, but Bob Brownley was the calmest of them all. It's the Exchange code that at any cost of heart or nerve-tear a man must retain good form until the gong strikes. Then, that he must be as near the uncaged tiger as human mind and body can be made. Only I realised what volcano raged inside my chum's bosom. If any other man of the crowd had known, Bob's chances of success would have been on par with a Canadian canoeist short-cutting Niagara for Buffalo. Nine-tenths of the Stock Exchange game is not letting your left brain-lobe know what race your right is in until the winning numbers and the also-rans are on the board. If one of those three hundred chain-lightning thinkers or any of their ten thousand alert associates knew in advance the intentions of a fellow broker, the word would sweep through that crowd with the sureness of uncorked ether, and the other two hundred and ninty nine, at gong-strike, would be at each others' throats for his vitals, and before he knew the game had started would have his bones picked to a vulture-finish cleanness. Suddenly, as I watched the scene, there rang through the great hall the first sharp stroke of the gong. There were no echoes heard that morning. The metallic voice was yet shaping its command to "at 'em, you fiends" when from three hundred throats burst the wild sound of the Stock Exchange yell. No other sound in any of the open or hidden places of all nature duplicates the yell of a great Stock Exchange at an exciting opening. It not only fills and refills space, for the volume is terrific, but it has an individuality all its own, coming from the incisive "take-mine-I've-got yours," from the aggressive, almost arrogant "you-can't-you-won't-have-your-way," the confident "by-heaven-I-will" individual notes that enter into the whole, as they blend with the shrill scream of triumph and the die-away note of disappointment, when the floor men realise their success or their failure. I picked Bob's magnificently resonant voice from the mass—"40 for any part of 10,000 Sugar." It was this daring bid that struck terror to the bears and filled the bulls[2] with a frenzy of encouragement. Again it rang out—"45 for any part of 25,000"; and a third time—"50 for any part of 50,000."

The great crowd was surging all over the room. Hats were smashed and coats were being stripped from their owners' backs as though made of paper, and now and then a particularly frantic buyer or seller would be borne to the floor by the impetus of those who sought to fill his bid or grab his offer. Through all the wild whirl, straight and erect and commanding was the form of Bob, his face cold and expressionless as an iceberg. In five minutes the human mass had worked back to the Sugar-pole and there was the inevitable lull while its members "verified."

FRIDAY, THE THIRTEENTH

I could see by the few entries Bob was making on his pad that he had been compelled to buy but little. This meant that his campaign was working smoothly, that he was driving the market up by merely bidding, and that he had the greater part of my 50,000 yet unbought, which inturn meant he could continue to push up the price, or in the event of his opponents' attempting to run it down, he would be under the market with big supporting orders.

Suddenly the lull was broken. Bob's voice rang out again—"153 for any part of 10,000 Sugar." Again the gamblers closed in and for another five minutes the opening scene was duplicated, with only a shade less fierceness. After ten minutes' mad trading a mighty burst of sound told that Sugar was 160 bid. Then Bob worked his way out of the crowd, and passing by me fairly hissed, "By heaven, Jim, I've got them cinched!"

I went back to the office. In a few minutes Bob without a word strode through my office and into the little room occupied by Beulah Sands. He closed the door behind him, a thing that he had never done before. It was only a minute till he opened it and called to me. In his eyes was a strange look, a look that came from the blending of two mighty passions, one joy, the other I could not make out, unless it was that soft one, which suppressed love, emerging from terrible uncertainty, generates in deep natures and which usually finds vent in tears. Beulah Sands was a study. Her heart was evidently swaying and tugging with the news Bob had brought her. She must have seen the nearness of release from the torture that had been filling her soul during the past three months, and yet such was the remarkable self-control of the woman, such her noble courage, that she refused to show any outward sign of her feelings. She was the reserved, dignified girl I had ever seen her. "Jim, Miss Sands and I thought it best that we should have a little match up at this stage of our deal," Bob began. "I want to know if you both agree with me on adhering to the original plans to close out at 175. I never felt surer of my ground than in this deal.

The stock is 163 on the tape right now." He glanced at the white paper ribbon whose every foot on certain days spells Heaven or Hell to countless mortals, as it rolled out of the ticker in the corner of the office. "Yes, there she goes again—3¾, 4, 4¼ and 1,200 at a half. There is a tremendous demand from all quarters. Washington's buying is unlimited; the commission-houses are tumbling over one another to get aboard and the shorts are scared to a paralysed muteness. They don't know whether to jump in and cover or to stand their present hands, but they have no pluck to fight the rise, that is certain. The news bureaus have just published the story that I am buying for Randolph & Randolph, and they for the insiders; that the new tariff is as good as passed; and that at the directors' meeting to-morrow the Sugar dividend will be increased, and that it is agreed on all sides she won't stop going until she crosses 200. I've been obliged to take on only 18,000 of your 50,000, and at present prices there is over two hundred thousand profit in them. I think I could go back there and in thirty minutes have it to 180. Then if I rested on it until about one o'clock and threw myself at it for real fireworks up to the close, I could, under cover of them, let slip about half our purchases, and to-morrow open her with a whirl and let go the balance. If I'm in luck I'll average 180-185 for the whole bunch, but I'll be satisfied if I get an average of 175, which would allow me to sell it on a dropping scale to 160."

I agreed that his campaign was perfect, and Beulah Sands said in her usual quiet way, "It is entirely in your hands, Mr. Brownley. I don't see how any advice from us can help."

Bob went back to the Exchange and I into my office. Bob had been right again. In ten minutes the tape began to scream Sugar. With enormous transactions it ran up in fifteen minutes to 188, in three more it dropped to 181, and then steadily mounted to 185½, dulled up, and was healthy steady. Presently Bob was back and we sat down again.

FRIDAY, THE THIRTEENTH

"I've bought 20,000 more for you, Jim, on that bulge. I've 38,000 in all of the last 50,000, which leaves me 12,000 reserve. The average is 'way under 75, and there must be $400,000 for you in it now and a strong $1,400,000 in Miss Sands's 20,000, and $1,800,000 in our 30,000. They say it's bad business to count chickens in the shell, but ours are tapping so hard to get out I can't help doing it this once. I'm going to keep away from the floor for an hour or so, then I will go over and wind it up and—good God, Beulah—Miss Sands—are you ill?"

The girl's face was ashen gray and she seemed to be gasping for breath. I rushed for some water while Bob seized both her hands, but in an instant the blood came to her cheeks with a rush and she said, "I was dizzy for a moment. It must have been the thought of taking $1,800,000 back to father that upset me. With that amount father could make good all the trust funds and have back enough of his own fortune to make us seem, after what we have been going through, richer than we were before. Pardon me, Mr. Randolph, won't you, when I say—God bless you and every one whom you hold dear, God bless you? What could I or my father have done but for you and Mr. Brownley?"

She turned her big eyes full upon Bob, filled with a light such as can come only to a woman's eyes, only to a woman before whom, as she stands on the brink of hell, suddenly looms her heaven.

Sharp and shrill rang Bob's Exchange telephone. The ring seemed shriller; it certainly was longer than usual. Bob jumped for the receiver.

Chapter III

HE LISTENED A moment, then answered, "Stand on it at 80 for 12,000 shares. I will be there in a second." He dropped the receiver. "Jim, we have struck a snag. Arthur Perkins, whom I left on guard at the pole, says Barry Conant has just jumped in and supplied all the bids. He has it down to 81 and is offering it in 5,000 blocks and is aggressive. I must get there quick," and he shot out of the office.

I sprang for Bob's telephone: "Perkins, quick!" "What are they doing, Perkins?" I asked a moment later.

"Conant has almost filled me up. He seems to have a hogshead of it on tap," he answered.

"Buy 50,000 shares, 5,000 each point down; and anything unfilled, give to Bob when he gets there. He is on the way."

I shut off, and turned to Miss Sands:

"This is no time to stand on ceremony, Miss Sands. Barry Conant is Camemeyer's and 'Standard Oil's' head broker. His being on the floor means mischief. He never goes into a big whirl personally unless they are out for blood. Bob has exhausted his buying power, and though I tell you frankly that I never speculate, don't believe in speculation and am in this deal only for Bob—and for you—I swear I don't intend to let them wipe the floor with him without at least making them swallow some of the dust they kick up. Please don't object to my helping out, Miss Sands. Ordinarily I would defer to your wishes, but I love Bob Brownley only second to my wife, and I have money enough to warrant a plunge in stock. If they should turn Bob over in this deal, he—well, they're not going to, if I can prevent it," and I started for the Exchange on the run.

When I got there the scene beggared description. That of the morning was tame in comparison. A bull market, however terrific, always is tame beside a bear crash. In the few moments it took me to get to the floor, the battle had started. The greater part of the Exchange membership was in a dense mob wedged against the rail behind the Sugar-pole. I could not have got within yards of the centre of that crowd of men, fast becoming panic-stricken, if the fate of nations had depended on my errand. I had witnessed such a scene before. It represented a certain phase of Stock-Exchange-gambling procedure, where one man apparently has every other man on the floor against him. I understood: Bob against them all—he trying to stay the onrushing current of dropping prices; they bent on keeping the sluice-gates open. He was backed up against the rail—not the Bob of the morning; not a vestige of that cold, brain-nerve-and-body-in-hand gambler remained. His hat was gone, his collar torn and hanging over his shoulder. His coat and waistcoat were ripped open, showing the full length of his white shirt-front, and his eyes were fairly mad. Bob was no longer a human being, but a monarch of the forest at bay, with the hunter in front of him, and closing in upon him, in a great half-circle, the pack of harriers, all gnashing their teeth, baring their fangs, and howling for blood. The hunter directly facing Bob, was Barry Conant—very slight, very short, a marvellously compact, handsome, miniature man, with a fascinating face, dark olive in tint, lighted by a pair of sparkling black eyes and framed in jet-black hair; a black mustache was parted over white teeth, which, when he was stalking his game, looked like those of a wolf. An interesting man at all times was this Barry Conant, and he had been on more and fiercer battle-fields than any other half-score members combined. The scene was a rare one for a student of animalised men.

While every other man in the crowd was at a high tension of excitement, Barry Conant was as calm as though standing in the centre of a ten-acre daisy-field cutting off the helpless flowers' heads with every swing of his arm. Switching stock-gamblers into eternity had grown to be a pastime to Barry Conant. Here was Bob thundering with terrific emphasis "78 for 5,000," "77 for 5,000," "75 for 5,000," "74 for 5,000," "73 for 5,000," "72 for 5,000," seemingly expecting through sheer power of voice to crush his opponent into silence. But with the regularity of a trip-hammer Barry Conant's right hand, raised in unhurried gesture, and his clear calm "Sold" met Bob's every retreating bid. It was a battle royal—a king on one side, a Richelieu on the other. Though there was frantic buying and selling all around these two generals, the trading was gauged by the trend of their battle. All knew that if Bob should be beaten down by this concentrated modern finance devil, a panic would ensue and Sugar would go none could say how low. But if Bob should play him to a standstill by exhausting his selling power, Sugar would quickly soar to even higher figures than before. It was known that Barry Conant's usual order from his clients, the "System" masters, for such an occasion as the present was "Break the price at any cost." On the other hand, every one knew that Randolph & Randolph were usually behind Bob's big operations; this was evidently one of his biggest; and every man there knew that Randolph & Randolph were seldom backed down by any force.

As Bob made his bid "72 for 5,000," and got it, I saw a quick flash of pain shoot across his face, and realised that it probably meant he was nearing the end of my last order. I sized it up that there was deviltry of more than usual significance behind this selling movement; that Barry Conant must have unlimited orders to sell and smash. My final order of fifty thousand brought our total up to one hundred and fifty thousand shares, a large amount for even Randolph & Randolph to buy of a stock selling at nearly $200 a share. I then and there decided that whatever happened I would go no further. Just then Bob's wild eye caught mine, and there was in it a piteous appeal, such an appeal as one sees in the eye of the wounded doe when she gives up her attempt to swim to shore and waits the coming of the pursuing hunter's canoe. I sadly signaled that I was through. As Bob caught the sign, he threw his head back and bellowed a deep, hoarse "70 for 10,000." I knew then that he had already bought forty thousand, and that this was the last-ditch stand. Barry Conant must have caught the meaning too. Instantly, like a revolver report, came his "Sold!" Then the compact, miniature mass of human springs and wires, which had until now been held in perfect control, suddenly burst from its clamps, and Barry Conant was the fiend his Wall Street reputation pictured him. His five feet five inches seemed to loom to the height of a giant. His arms, with their fate-pointing fingers, rose and fell with bewildering rapidity as his piercing voice rang out—"5,000 at 69, 68, 65," "10,000 at 63," "25,000 at 60." Pandemonium reigned. Every man in the crowd seemed to have the capital stock of the Sugar Trust to sell, and at any price. A score seemed to be bent on selling as low as possible instead of for as much as they could get. These were the shorts who had been punished the day before by Bob's uplift.

Poor Bob, he was forgotten! An instant after he made his last effort he was the dead cock in the pit. Frenzied gamblers of the Stock Exchange have no more use for the dead cocks than have Mexicans for the real birds when they get the fatal gaff. The day after the contest, or even that same night at Delmonico's and the clubs, these men would moan for poor Bob; Barry Conant's moan would be the loudest of them all, and, what is more, it would be sincere. But on battle day away to the dump with the fallen bird, the bird that could not win! I saw a look of deep, terrible agony spread over Bob's face; and then in a flash he was the Bob Brownley who I always boasted had the courage and the brain to do the right thing in all circumstances. To the astonishment of every man in the crowd he let loose one wild yell, a cross between the war-whoop of an Indian and the bay of a deep-lunged hound regaining a lost scent. Then he began to throw over Sugar stock, right and left, in big and little amounts. He slaughtered the price, under-cutting Barry Conant's every offer and filling every bid. For twenty minutes he was a madman, then he stopped. Sugar was falling rapidly to the price it finally reached, 90, and the panic was in full swing, but panics seemed now to have no interest for Bob. He pushed his way through the crowd and, joining me, said: "Jim, forgive me. I have dragged you into an enormous loss, have ruined Beulah Sands, her father, and myself. I think at the last moment I did the only thing possible. I threw over the 150,000 shares and so cut off some of our loss. Let us go to the office and see where we stand." He was strangely, unnaturally calm after that heart-crushing, nerve-tearing day. I tried to tell him how I admired his cool nerve and pluck in about-facing and doing the only thing there was left to do; to tell him that required more real courage and level-headedness than all the rest of the day's doings; but he stopped me:

"Jim, don't talk to me. My conceit is gone. I have learned my lesson to-day. My plans were all right, and sound, but poor fool that I was, I did not take into consideration the loaded dice of the master thieves. I knew what they could do, have seen them scores of times, as you have, at their slaughter; seen them crush out the hearts of other men just as good as you or I; seen them take them out and skin and quarter-slice them, unmindful of the agony of those who were dear to and dependent on their owners, but it never seemed to strike me home. It was not my heart, and somehow, I looked at it as a part of the game and let it go at that. To-day I know what it means to be put on the chopping-block of the 'System' butchers. I know what it is to see my heart and the heart of one I love—and yours, too, Jim—systematically skewered to those of the hundreds and thousands of victims who have gone before. Jim, we must be three millions losers, and the men who have our money have so many, many millions that they can't live long enough even to thumb them over. Men who will use our money on the gambling-table, at the race-tracks, squander it on stage harlots, or in turning their wives and daughters or their neighbours' wives and daughters into worse than stage harlots. Men, Jim, who are not fit, measured by any standard of decency, to walk the same earth as you and Judge Sands. Men whose painted pets pollute the very air that such as

Beulah Sands must breathe. I've learned my lesson to-day. I thought I knew the game of finance, but I'm suddenly awakened to a realisation of the dense ignorance I wallowed in. Jim, but for the loading of the dice, I should now have been taking Beulah Sands to her father with the money that the hellish 'System' stole from him. Later I should have taken her to the altar, and after, who knows but that I should have had the happiest home and family in all the world, and lived as her people and mine have lived for generations, honest, God-fearing, law-abiding, neighbour-loving men and women, and then died as men should die? But now, Jim, I see a black, awful picture. No, I'm not morbid, I'm going to make a heroic effort to put the picture out of sight; but I'm afraid, Jim, I'm afraid."

He stopped as we pulled up on the sidewalk in front of Randolph & Randolph's office. "Here it is on the bulletin. See what did the trick, Jim. They held the Sugar meeting last night instead of waiting till to-morrow, and cut the dividend instead of increasing it. The world won't know it until to-morrow. Then they will know it, then they will know it. They will read it in the headlines of the papers—a few suicides, a few defaulters, a few new convicts, an unclaimed corpse or two at the morgue; a few innocent girls, whose fathers' fortunes have gone to swell Camemeyer's and 'Standard Oil's' already uncountable gold, turned into streetwalkers; a few new palaces on Fifth Avenue, and a few new libraries given to communities that formerly took pride in building them from their honestly earned savings. A report or two of record-breaking diamond sales by Tiffany to the kings and czars of dollar royalty, then front-page news stories of clawing, mauling, and hair-pulling wrangles among the stage harlots for the possession of these diamonds. They were not quite sure that the dividend cut alone would do the trick, and they were taking no chances, these mighty warriors of the 'System,' so their hireling Senate committee held a session last night and unanimously reported to put sugar on the free list. The people will read that in the morning, and probably the day after they'll be told that the committee held another session to-night and unanimously reported to take it off the free list. By that time these honourable statesmen will have loaded up with the stock that you and I and Beulah Sands sold, and that other poor devils will slaughter to-morrow after reading their morning papers."

Bob's bitterness was terrible. My heart was torn as I listened. He stalked through the office and into that of Beulah Sands. I followed. She was at her desk, and when she looked up, her great eyes opened in wonderment as they took in Bob, his grim, set face, the defiant, sullen desperation of the big brown eyes, the dishevelled hair and clothes. For an instant she stood as one who had seen an apparition.

"Look me over, Beulah Sands," he said, "look me over to your heart's content, for you may never again see the fool of fools in all the world, the fool who thought himself competent to cope with men of brains, with men who really know how to play the game of dollars as it is played in this Christian age. Don't ask me not to call you Beulah; that what I tried to do was for you is the one streak of light in all this black hell. Beulah, Beulah, we are ruined, you, your father, and I, ruined, and I'm the fool who did it."

She rose from her desk with all the quiet, calm dignity that we had been admiring for three months, and stood facing Bob. She did not seem to see me; she saw nothing but the man who had gone out that morning the personification of hope, who now stood before her the picture of black despair, and she must have thought, "It was all for me." Suddenly she took the lapels of his torn coat in either hand. She had to reach up to do it, this winsome little Virginia lady. With her big calm blue eyes looking straight into his, she said:

"Bob."

That was all, but the word seemed to change the very atmosphere in the room. The look of desperation faded from Bob's face, and as though the words had sprung the hidden catch to the doors of his storehouse of pent-up misery, his eyes filled with hot, blinding tears. His great chest was convulsed with sobs. Again—clear, calm, fearless, and tender, came the one syllable, "Bob." And at that Bob's self-control slipped the leash. With a hoarse cry, he threw his arms around her and crushed her to his breast. The sacredness of the scene made me feel like an intruder, and I started to leave the room. But in a moment Beulah Sands was her usual self and, turning to me, she said: "Mr. Randolph, please forget what you have seen. For an instant, as I saw Mr. Brownley's awful misery, I thought of nothing but what he had done for me, what he had tried to do for my father, what a penalty he has paid. From what you said when you left and the fact that I got no word from either of you, I feared the worst and did not dare look at the tape; I simply waited and hoped and—prayed. Yes, I prayed as my mother taught me I should pray whenever I was helpless and could do nothing myself. And I felt that God would not let the noble work of two such men be overthrown by those you were battling with. In the midst of a calmness that I took for a good omen, you came. Can you blame me for forgetting myself? Mr. Brownley," the voice was now calm and self-controlled, "tell me what you have done. Where do we stand?" "There is little to tell," Bob answered. "Camemeyer and 'Standard Oil' have taken me into camp as they would take a stuck pig. They have made a monkeyfied ass out of me, and we are ruined, and I have caused Mr. Randolph a heavy loss. Roughly, I figure that of your four hundred thousand capital and the million four hundred thousand profit you had this morning, only your capital remains."

Wishing to spare Bob, I interrupted and myself gave the girl briefly the details of what had happened. She listened intently and seemed to take in all the trickery of the "System" masters; seemed to see just what it meant to us and to her. But she made no comment, showed by no outward sign that she suffered. As soon as I was through she turned to Bob, who had stood with his eyes fastened upon her face, as though somewhere out of its soft beauty must come an assurance that this was all a bad dream.

"Mr. Brownley," she said, "let us figure up just where we stand, so that we may know what to do to recoup. You have said so many times, since I have been here, that Wall Street is magic land; that no man may tell twenty-four hours ahead what will happen to him. You have said it so many times that I believe it. We know that this morning we were at the goal, that we were millions ahead, and all from twenty-four hours' effort. We have yet almost three months left, and I do not see why we have not just as much chance as we had day before yesterday. Yes, and more, because we know more now. Next time we will include the dividend cuts and the Senate duplicity in our figuring."

We both dumbly stared in wondering admiration at this marvellous woman. Was it possible that a girl could have such nerve, such courage? Or had woman's hope, so persistent where her loved ones are concerned, made Beulah Sands blind to the awfulness of the situation? As I looked at her I could not doubt that she fully realised our position, that she was really suffering more than either of us, that she was only acting to ease Bob's anguish. Bob brought out his memoranda, and in half an hour we had the figures. The total loss was nearly three millions. As Beulah Sands's 20,000 shares had cost less than ours and Bob figured to leave her capital of $400,000 intact, we felt some comfort. Beulah Sands had watched the figuring with the keenness of an expert, and when Bob announced the final figures, which showed that she still had what she started with, she drew the sheet containing the totals to her. "I was willing to accept your assistance," she said, "when the deal promised a profit to all of us, because I appreciated your goodness and knew how much it would hurt your feelings if I were churlish about the division; but now that we all lose I must stand my fair share; I must." She said this in a way that we both knew precluded the possibility of argument. "We owned together 150,000 shares. I was to have had the profits on 20,000 shares. Our total loss is $2,775,000, of which I must bear my just proportion. Mr. Brownley, you will see that $370,000 is charged to my account. I shall have $30,000 left. If our cause is as just as we think, God in his goodness will make this ample for our purposes."

Though Bob and I were in despair at her determination to strip herself of what Bob had worked so hard to accumulate, we could not help feeling a reverence for her faith and her sturdy independence. She now showed us in her delicate way that she wished to be alone; as we went she held out her hand to Bob. "Mr. Brownley, please, for the sake of the work we have to do, look on the bright side of this calamity, for it has a bright side. You wanted me to send word to my father that we were about to grasp victory. Think if we had sent it—then you will know that God is good, even when we think he is chastening us beyond endurance."

Bob took me into his office. "Jim, you see what a woman can do, and we are taught women are the weaker sex. Now listen to what you must do. Accept my notes for the whole loss, less one hundred thousand which I have to my credit, and which I will pay on account. I won't listen to any objection. The deal was mine; you came in only to help us out, and I ought never to have tempted you. If I remain in my present busted condition, the notes will be blank paper. Therefore you do me no harm in taking them. If I should strike it rich, I should never feel like a man until I made up the loss."

It was no use arguing with him in his inflexible mood, so I took his demand notes for $2,405,000. I begged him to go home with me to dinner, but he insisted that he could not face my wife with his last night's break still fresh in her mind. Next day he did not turn up. Along in the afternoon I received a telegram from him, saying that he was on his way to Virginia, that he needed a rest and would be back in a week. I was worried, nervous. It takes until the next day and the day after, and the week after that, to get down to the deepest misery of an upset such as we had been through. I did not feel easy with Bob out of sight while he was sounding for a new footing. I went to Beulah Sands in hope we might talk over the affair, but when I told her that Bob was to be gone for a week and that I was uneasy, she said in her calm, confident manner: "I don't think there is anything to worry about, Mr. Randolph. Mr. Brownley is too much of a man to allow an affair of dollars to do anything more than annoy him. He will be back all the better for his rest." She dropped her long lashes in a this-conversation-is-closed way that we had come to know meant going time.

Chapter IV

THE FOLLOWING WEEK Bob returned to the office. He had not changed, and yet he had changed greatly. Rest had apparently done much for him. His colour was good, his step elastic as of old, and his head was thrown back as if he were buckled up for the fray and wanted all to know it. Yet there was something in the eye, in the setness of the jaw, in the hair-trigger calm, yet fiercely savage grip in which he closed his strong hands on the arms of his chair, that told me more plainly than words that this was not the optimistic, soft-hearted Bob Brownley I had known and loved. I could not help feeling that if I had been a leader of the Russian terrorists, and this man who now sat before me had come to my ken when I was selecting bomb-throwers, I should have seized upon him of all men as the one to stalk the Czar or his marked minions. Surely the iron that had entered Bob's soul a week before had affected his whole being. I think Beulah Sands had some such thoughts. For I saw a shadow of perplexity cross her broad, low forehead after her first meeting with him, a shadow that had not been there before.

For days after Bob's return I saw little of him. I think Beulah Sands saw less. During Stock Exchange hours he spent most of his time on the floor, but he executed few of our orders. He merely looked them over and handed them out to his assistants. As far as I could learn, he spent much of his time there yesterdaying through hope's graveyards, a not uncommon pastime for active Exchange members whose first through specials have been open-switched by the "System" towerman. So strong had become this habit of going about from pole to pole with bent head and a far-off gaze that his fellow members began to humour and respect it. They all knew that Bob had gone up against the Sugar panic hard. No one knew how hard, but all guessed from his changed appearance and habits that it must have been a bone-smashing blow. Nothing so quickly and so deeply stirs a Stock Exchange man's feelings for his brother member as to know that "They" have ditched his El Dorado flyer—that is, if he has been a good the books showed no change in Beulah Sands's account. There was the poor little $30,000 balance; no other entries. One afternoon Beulah Sands had asked for a meeting between Bob and myself in her office. She could hardly have asked Bob to come without me, but I knew it was Bob she wanted to see, and I felt that the best thing I could do for them was to leave them alone. So I made some excuse for a moment's delay at my desk, telling Bob to go on into her office, and promising to follow shortly. He went in, leaving the door partly open. I think that from the moment he entered the room both of them utterly forgot my existence. From her desk Beulah could not see me, and Bob sat so that his back was half toward me. "I dislike to trouble you about my account," I heard her begin in a voice a trifle uneven, "but as I must go back to Father Christmas week, I wanted to get your advice as to the advisability of writing him that, though there is still a chance for doing wonders, I do not think we shall be able to save him. Of course I won't put it in just that blunt way, but it seems to me I should begin to prepare him for the blow. I have not talked over any more plunging with you, Mr. Brownley, since the unlucky one in Sugar, and——"

"Miss Sands, I understand what you mean," Bob broke in, "and I should apologise for not having consulted with you about your business affairs. The fact is, I have not been quite clear as to the best thing to do. I hope you don't think I have forgotten. Never for a moment since I took charge of your affairs have I forgotten my promise to see that they were kept active. Truly I have been trying to think out some successful plunge, but—but"—there was a hoarseness in his voice—"I have not had my old confidence in myself since that day in Sugar when I killed your hopes and destroyed the chance of saving your father—no, I have not had that confidence a man must have in himself to win at this game."

FRIDAY, THE THIRTEENTH

There was a silence, and then I heard an indescribable fluttering rush that told as plainly as sight could have done that a woman had answered her heart's call. Looking up involuntarily, I saw a sight that for a long moment held my eyes as if I had been fascinated. It was Bob bowed forward with his face hidden in his hands and beside him, on her knees, Beulah Sands, her arms about his neck, his head drawn down to her bosom. "Bob, Bob," she said chokingly, "I cannot stand it any longer. My heart is breaking for you. You were so happy when I came into your life, and the happiness is changed to misery and despair, and all for me, a stranger. At first I thought of nothing but father and how to save him, but since that day when those men struck at your heart, I have been filled with, oh! such a longing to tell you, to tell you, Bob——"

"What? Beulah, what? For the love of God, don't stop; tell me, Beulah, tell me." He had not lifted his head. It was buried on her breast, his arms closed around her. She bent her head and laid her beautiful, soft cheek, down which the tears were now streaming, against his brown hair. "Bob, forgive me, but I love you, love you, Bob, as only a woman can love who has never known love before, never known anything but stern duty. Bob, night after night when all have left I have crept into your office and sat in your chair. I have laid my head on your desk and cried and cried until it seemed as though I could not live till morning without hearing you say that you loved me, and that you did not mind the ruin I had brought into your life. I have patted the back of your chair where your dear head had rested. I have covered the arms of your chair, that your strong, brave hands had gripped, with kisses. Night after night I have knelt at your desk and prayed to God to shield you, to protect you from all harm, to brush away the black cloud I brought into your life. I have asked Him to do with me, yes, with my father and mother, anything, anything if only He would bring back to you the happiness I had stolen. Bob, I have suffered, suffered, as only a woman can suffer."

61

She was sobbing as though her heart would break, sobbing wildly, convulsively, like the little child who in the night comes to its mother's bed to tell of the black goblins that have been pursuing it. Long before she had finished speaking—and it took only a few heart-beats for that rush of words—I had broken the power of the fascination that held me, had turned away my eyes, and tried not to listen. For fear of breaking the spell, I did not dare cross the room to close Beulah's door or to reach the outer door of my office, which was nearer hers than it was to my desk. I waited—through a silence, broken only by Beulah's weeping, that seemed hour-long. Then in Bob's voice came one low sob of joy:

"Beulah, Beulah, my Beulah!"

I realised that he had risen. I rose too, thinking that now I could close the door. But again I saw a picture that transfixed me. Bob had taken Beulah by both shoulders and he held her off and looked into her eyes long and beseechingly. Never before nor since have I seen upon human face that glorious joy which the old masters sought to get into the faces of their worshippers who, kneeling before Christ, tried to send to Him, through their eyes, their soul's gratitude and love. I stood as one enthralled. Slowly and as reverently as the living lover touches the brow of his dead wife, Bob bent his head and kissed her forehead. Again and again he drew her to him and implanted upon her brow and eyes and lips his kisses. I could not stand the scene any longer. I started to the corridor-door, and then, as though for the first time either had known I was within hearing, they turned and stared at me. At last Bob gave a long deep sigh, then one of those reluctant laughs of happiness yet wet with sobs.

"Well, Jim, dear old Jim, where did you come from? Like all eavesdroppers, you have heard no good of yourself. Own up, Jim, you did not hear a word good or bad about yourself, for it is just coming back to me that we have been selfish, that we have left you entirely out of our business conference."

We all laughed, and Beulah Sands, with her face a bloom of burning blushes, said: "Mr. Randolph, we have not settled what it is best to do about father's affairs."

After a little we did begin to talk business, and finally agreed that Beulah should write her father, wording her letter as carefully as possible, to avoid all direct statements, but showing him that she had made but little headway on the work she had come North to accomplish. Bob was a changed being now; so, too, was Beulah Sands. Both discussed their hopes and fears with a frankness in strange contrast to their former manner. But there was one point on which Bob showed he was holding back. I finally put it to him bluntly: "Bob, are you working out anything that looks like real relief for Miss Sands and her father?"

"I don't know how to answer you, Jim. I can only say I have some ideas, radical ones perhaps, but—well, I am thinking along certain lines."

I saw he was not yet willing to take us into his confidence. We parted, Bob going along in the cab with Miss Sands.

Two days afterward she sent for us both as soon as we got to the office.

"I have this telegram from father—it makes me uneasy: 'Mailed to-day important letter. Answer as soon as you receive.'"

The following afternoon the letter came. It showed Judge Sands in a very nervous, uneasy state. He said he had been living a life of daily terror, as some of his friends, for whose estates he was trustee, had been receiving anonymous letters, advising them to look into the judge's trust affairs; that the Reinhart crowd had been using renewed pressure to make him let go all his Seaboard stock, which they wanted to secure at the low prices to which they had depressed it, in order that they might reorganise and carry out the scheme they had been so long planning. Judge Sands went on to say that the day he was compelled to sell his Seaboard stock he would have to make public an announcement of his condition, as there could be no sale without the court's consent. His closing was:

> "My dear daughter, no one knows better than I the almost hopelessness of expecting any relief from your operations. But so hopeless have I become of late, so much am I reliant upon you, my dear child, and eternal hope so springs in all of us when confronted with great necessities, that I have hoped and still hope that you are to be the saviour of your family; that you, only a frail child, are through God's marvellous workings to be the one to save the honour of that name we both love more than life; the one to keep the wolf of poverty from that door through which so far has come nothing but the sunshine of prosperity and happiness; the one, my dear Beulah, who is to save your old father from a dishonoured grave. Dear child, forgive me for placing upon your weak shoulders the additional burden of knowing I am now helpless and compelled to rely absolutely upon you. After you have read my letter, if there is no hope, I command you to tell me so at once, for although I am now financially and almost mentally helpless, I am still a Sands, and there has never yet been one of the name who shirked his duty, however stern and painful it might be."

When I handed the letter back to Miss Sands, she said:

"Mr. Randolph, let me tell you and Mr. Brownley a little about my father and our home, that you may see our situation as it is. My father is one of the noblest men that ever lived. I am not the only one who says that—if you were to ask the people of our State to name the one man who had done most for the State as a State, most for her progressive betterment, most for her people high and low, white and black, they would answer, 'Judge Lee Sands.' He has been, and is, the idol of our people. After he was graduated from Harvard, he entered the law office of my grandfather, Senator Robert Lee Sands. Before he was thirty he was in Congress and was even then reputed the greatest orator of our State, where orators are so plentiful. He married my mother, his second cousin, Julia Lee, of Richmond, at twenty-five, and from then until the attack of that ruthless money-shark, led a life such as a true man would map out for himself if his Maker granted him the privilege. You would have to visit at our home to appreciate my father's character and to understand how terrible this sorrow is to him. Every morning of his life he spends an hour after breakfast with my dear mother, who is a cripple from hip disease. He takes her in his arms and brings her down from her room to the library as if she were a child. He then reads to her—and he knows good books as well as he knows his friends. After he takes mother back to her room, he gives an hour to our people, the blacks of the plantation and his white tenants throughout the county. He is a father to them all. He settles all their troubles, big and little. Then for hours he and I go over his business affairs. Every afternoon from four to five he devotes to his estates and the men and women for whom he acts as trustee. He has often said to me: 'We have a clear million of money and property, and that is all any man should have in America. It is all he is entitled to under our form of government. Any more than that an honest man should in one way or another return to the people from whom he has taken it. I never want my family to have more than a million dollars.' When he went into the Seaboard affair, he explained to me that it was to assist the Wilsons—they were old friends, and he has acted as their solicitor for years—in building up the South. He discussed with me the right and advisability of putting in the trust funds. He said he considered it his duty to employ them as he did his own in enterprises that would aid the whole people of the South, instead of sending them to the North to be used in Wall Street as belting for the 'System' grinder. These fortunes were made in the South by men who loved their section of the country more than they did wealth, and why should they not be employed to benefit that part of the country which their makers and owners loved? I remember vividly how perplexed he was when, at the beginning, the Wilsons would show him that the investments were returning unusually large profits.

"'It is not right, Beulah,' he said to me one morning after receiving a letter from Baltimore to the effect that Seaboard stock and bonds had advanced until his investment showed over fifty per cent, profit, 'it is not right for us to make this money. No man in America should make over legal rates of interest and a fair profit on an investment, that is, an investment of capital pure and simple, particularly in a transportation company, where every dollar of profit comes from the people who patronise the lines. I have worked it out on every side, and it is not right; it would not be legal if the people, who make the laws for their own betterment, understood their affairs as they should.'

"He was always writing to the Wilsons to conduct the affairs of the Seaboard so that there would be remaining each year only profits enough to keep the road up and the wharves in good condition and to pay the annual interest and a fair dividend. And when the Wilsons came to our house to lay before him the offer of Reinhart and his fellow plunderers to pay enormous profits for the control of the Seaboard, he was indignant and argued with them that the offer was an insult to honest men. It was he who advised the trusteeship control of the Seaboard stock to prevent Reinhart from securing control. I sat in the library when he talked to the elder Wilson and the directors.

"He appealed directly to John Wilson to make an effort to stop the growing tendency to use the people as pawns to enslave themselves and their children. He said some man of undoubted probity, standing, and wealth, someone whom the people trusted, must start the fight against these New York fiends, whose only thought is to roll up wealth. And he told John Wilson he was the man, since he had great wealth, honestly got by his father and grandfather; no one would accuse him of being a hypocrite, seeking notoriety, and his standing in the financial world was so old and solid that it would have to listen to him. I remember-how emphatically father said: 'I tell you, John, *even the discussion* of such a proposition as that scoundrel Reinhart makes is degrading to an American's honour.' He said it didn't make the least difference if Reinhart counted his millions by the score, and was director in thirty or forty great institutions, and gave a fortune every year for charity and to the church—that he was a blackleg just the same. And so is any man, he said, who dares to say he will take the stock of a transportation company, which represents a certain amount of money invested, and double or multiply it by five and ten, simply because he can compel the people to pay exorbitant fares and freight-rates and so get profits on this fraudulently increased capital.

"It was the decision arrived at by father and the Wilsons at this meeting, a decision to refuse in any circumstances to allow our Southern people to be bled by the Wall Street 'System,' that started Reinhart and his dollar-fiends on the war-path. You can see from what I tell you of my father the terrible condition he is in now. At night, when I get to thinking of him, hoping against hope, with no one to help him, no one with whom he can talk over his affairs, when I think of his nobleness in devoting his time to mother and by sheer will-power concealing from her his awful suffering, it nearly drives me mad."

"Miss Sands, why will you not let me lend you the money necessary to tide your father over for a while?" I asked.

67

"You are so good, Mr. Randolph, but you don't quite understand my father in spite of what I have said. He would not relieve his suffering at the expense of another, not if it were a hundred times more acute. You cannot understand the old-fashioned, deep-rooted pride of the Sands."

"But can you not, at least temporarily, disguise from him just how you have arranged the relief?"

Her big blue eyes stared at me in bewilderment.

"Mr. Randolph, I could not deceive father. I could not tell him a lie even to save his life. It would be impossible. My father abhors a lie. He believes a man or woman who would lie the lowest of the low things on earth. When I go back to my father he will say, 'Tell me what you have done.' I can just see him now, standing between the big white pillars at the end of the driveway. I can hear him say calmly, 'Beulah, my daughter, welcome. Your mother is waiting for you in her room. Do not lose a moment getting to her.' Afterward he'll take me over the plantation to show me all the familiar things, and not one word will he allow me to say about our affairs until dinner is over, until the neighbours have left, for no Sands returns from long absence without a fitting home welcome. When I have said good night to mother and sister and he has drawn up my rocker in front of his big chair in the library alcove and I've lighted his cigar for him, he will look me in the eye and say, 'Daughter, tell me all you have done.' I would no more think of holding anything back than I would of stabbing him to the heart. No, Mr. Randolph, there is no possibility of relief except in fairly using that $30,000, and fairly winning back what Wall Street has stolen from father. Even that will cause both of us many twinges of conscience, and anything more is impossible. If this cannot be done, father must, all of us must, pay the penalty of Reinhart's ruthless act."

Bob had listened, but made no comment until she was through; then he said, "It looks to me as though the market is shaping up so that we may be able to do something soon." It was evident to both of us that he had some plan in mind.

Later we learned that that night Beulah wrote her father a long letter, telling him what she had done; that she had made almost two millions profit from her operations, that they had been lost, and that the outlook was not reassuring. She begged him to prepare himself for the final calamity; promising that if there were no change for the better by December 1st, she would come home to be with him when the blow fell. She begged him to prepare to meet it like a Sands, and assured him that if worse came to worst she would earn enough to keep poverty away. Judge Sands would receive this letter the second day following, Friday, the 13th day of November. My God! how well I know the date. It is seared into my brain as though with a white-hot iron.

After our talk with Beulah Sands I begged Bob to dine with me and go over matters at length to see if we could not find a way out to relief.

"No, Jim, I have work to do to-night, worn that won't wait. That Tariff Bill was buttoned up to-day, and it has just been announced that the Sugar directors have declared a big extra stock dividend. Things have come out just about as I told you they would, and the stock is climbing to-day. They say it will touch 200 to-morrow and 'the Street' is predicting 250 for it in ten days. Barry Conant has been a steady buyer all day and the news bureaus announced that Camemeyer and the 'Standard Oil' are twenty millions winners. They say the Washington gamblers, the Congressmen, Senators, and Cabinet members with their heelers and lobbyists have made a killing. About every one seems to have fattened up, Jim, but you and me and Beulah Sands and the public. The public gets the axe both ways as usual. They have been shaken out of their stock, and they will be compelled to pay millions more each year for their sugar than they would if this law had not been made for their benefit. Jim, there is no disguising the fact that the American people are as helpless in the hands of these thugs of the 'System' as though they lived in the realm of the Sultan, where a few cutthroat brigands are licensed to rob and oppress to their heart's content. Jim Randolph, you know this game of finance. You know how it is worked and the men who work it. Tell me if there is any consideration due Wall Street and its heart-and-soul butchers at the hands of honest men."

"I don't know what you mean, Bob. What are you driving at?"

"Never mind what I am driving at. I ask you whether, if an honest man knew how to beat Wall Street at its own game, he should hesitate to beat it—hesitate because of anything connected with conscience or morals? You saw what Barry Conant was able to do to us that day simply by standing on the floor of the Stock Exchange and outstaying me in opening and closing his mouth. You saw he was able to sell Sugar to a point so low that I was obliged to let go of our 150,000 shares at eight to ten million dollars less than we could have got for them if we could have held them until to-day. Because of this trick his clients, the 'System,' instead of us, make five to seven millions."

"I don't follow you, Bob. I know that Barry Conant was able to do this because he had more money behind him than you."

"You think so, do you, Jim? That is the way it looks to you, but I tell you money had nothing to do with it. Nothing had to do with it but the fiendish system of fraud and trickery upon which the whole stock-gambling structure is reared. Nothing entered into the whole business but the trickery of stock-gambling as conducted to-day. It was only a question, Jim, of a man's opening and closing his mouth and spitting out words. From the minute Barry Conant came into that crowd until he left and we were ruined, he showed no money, no anything that I did not show. From the very nature of the business he could not. He simply said 'Sold' oftener and longer than I said 'Buy.' He may have had money back of him, or he may only have had nerve. God Almighty is the only one who can tell, for when Conant was through he was able to buy back at 90 the 50,000 shares he sold me at 175, the 50,000 that broke my back. Jim, if I had known as much that day as I do now I would have stood in that crowd and bought all the stock he sold at 180 and I would have stood there buying until hell froze over or he quit; then I would have made him rebuy it at 280 or 2,080, and I would have broken him and all his Camemeyer and 'Standard Oil' backers; broken them to their last crime-covered dollar."

"Bob, what are you talking about? It is all Chinese to me. I cannot get head or tail of what you are driving at."

"I know you can't, Jim, neither could Wall Street if it were listening to me. But you will, and Wall Street will too, before many days go by. Now I must be off. I have work to do."

He put on his hat and left me trying to puzzle out just what he meant.

Next day the Sugar bulls had the centre of the Stock Exchange stage. All day long they tossed Sugar from one to another as though each thousand shares had been a wisp of hay instead of $200,000—for soon after the opening it soared to 200. The "System's" cohorts were in absolute control, with Barry Conant never a minute away from the Sugar-pole, always on the alert to steer the course of prices when they threatened to run away on the up or the down side. It was evident to the expert readers of the tape that the "System" was currying its steed for an exceptionally brilliant run. Ike Bloomstein, the Average Fiend, who for forty years had kept close track of every movement on the floor, and who would bet anything, from his Fifth Avenue mansion to his overripe boardroom straw hat, that all stocks and movements were as strictly subject to the law of averages as are the tides to the moon and sun, remarked to Joe Barnes, the loan expert:

"'Cam' unt de Keroseners are pudding up egstra dop rails to dot wool-pen deh haf ben pilding since deh took Pop Prownlee and deh Rantolphs into gamp. Unless my topesheet goes pack on me, for deh first dime in forty years dere vill pe a record clip pefore a veek from to-tay."

"I am with you there, Ike," answered Joe. "If Barry Conant's knife-edged teeth ever spelt a killin', they do to-day. I just got orders from somewhere to drop call money from four to two and a half per cent., and they have given me ten millions to drop it with and the order is to favour Sugar as 'collat.' Some one is anxious to make it easy for the bleaters to get the coin to buy all the Sugar they want. Ike, you and I might make turkey money for Thanksgiving if we only knew whether Barry and his bunch were going to shoot her up thirty or forty points before they turned the bag upside down, or whether they will bury them from 200 to 150. What do you think?"

"I gant make out, aldo I haf vatched dem sharp all day. Dey certainly haf deh lambs lined up right now for any vey dey vont to twist id. I nefer see a petter market for a deluge. From Barry's movements all day I should say dey vould keep hoistin' her until apout noon to-morrow, unt dat deh might get her up to two-tirty or even to deh two-fifty. Put dere are von or two topes on deh sheet vhat run deh uder vay. First der is dey fact you gant run out, dat dere is alreaty on deh Sugar vagon deh piggest load of chuicy suckers dat efer game in from deh suppurbs. Sharley Pates says if any von hat tapped his Vashington vire er any utter Capitol vire dis veek he vould haf tought dere vas a Senate, House, unt Kabinet roll-gall on. Deh topes say 'Cam' vill nefer led dat fat punch off grafters slite out mit real money if he gan help id unt deh game iss endirely in his hands."

"I agree with you, Ike. If I had the steering of this killing I don't think I would take any chance of tempting them to dump and grab the profits by carrying it much over 200. But you can't tell what 'Cam' and those four-eyed dentists at 26 Broadway will do."

"Yes, put der iss anudder t'ing, Cho, dat makes me sit up unt plink about her goin' ofer two hundred. To-morrow's Friday der t'irteenth."

"Of course, Ike, that is something to be reckoned with, and every man on the floor and in the Street as well has his eye on it. Friday, the 13th, would break the best bull market ever under way. You and I know that, Ike, and the dope shows it too, but you have got to stack this up against it on this trip: no man on the floor knows what Friday the 13th, means better than Barry Conant. He has worked it to the queen's taste many a time. Why, Barry would not eat to-day for fear the food would get stuck in his windpipe. He's never left the pole for a minute; but suppose, Ike, Barry has tipped off 'Cam' that all the boys will let go their fliers, and most of them will take one on the short side over to-night for a superstition drop at the opening; and suppose 'Cam' has told him to take them all into camp and give her a rafter-scraper at the opening, where would old Friday, 13th, land on to-morrow's dope-sheets? Bring up the average, wouldn't it, for five years to come? I tell you, Ike, she's too deep for me this run, and I'm goin' to let her alone and pay for the turkey out of loan commissions or stick to plain workday food."

"Zame here, Cho. Say, Cho, haf you noticed Pop Prownlee to-tay? He has frozen to deh fringe off dat Sugar crowd ess t'ough some von hat nipped 'is scarf-pin unt he vos layin' for him ass he game out. He hasn't made a trade to-tay unt yet he sticks like a stamp-tax. I ben keeping my eyes on him for I t'ought he hat someding up his sleeve dat might raise tust ven he tropt id. I dink Parry has hat deh same itear. He never loses sight of him, yet Pop hasn't made a trade to-tay, unt here id iss twenty minutes of der glose unt dere iss Parry in deh centre again whooping her up ofer two hundred unt four."

Chapter V

THURSDAY, NOVEMBER 12TH, was a memorable day in Wall Street. As the gong pealed its the-game's-closed-till-another-day, the myriad of tortured souls that are supposed to haunt the treacherous bogs and quicksands of the great Exchange, where lie their earthly hopes, must have prayed with renewed earnestness for its destruction before the morrow. Never had the Stock Exchange folded its tents with surer confidence of continuing its victorious march. Sugar advanced with record-breaking total sales to 207½ and in the final half-hour carried the whole list of stocks up with it. In that time some of the railroads jumped ten points. Sugar closed at the very top amid great excitement, with Barry Conant taking all offered. During the last thirty minutes it had become evident to all that the boardroom traders and plungers, together with many of the semi-professional gamblers, who operated through commission houses, were selling out their long stock and going short over the opening of the Wall Street hoodoo-day, Friday, the thirteenth of the month. But it was also evident, with the heavy selling at the close and the stiffness of the price, which had never wavered as block after block was thrown on the market, that some powerful interest as well had taken cognisance of the fact that the morrow was hoodoo-day. At the close, most of the sellers, had they been granted another five minutes, would have repurchased, even at a loss, what they had sold, for it looked as though they had sold themselves into a trap. Their anxiety was intensified by the publication, a few minutes later, of this item:

"Barry Conant in coming from the Sugar crowd after the close remarked to a fellow broker, 'By three o'clock to-morrow, Friday, the 13th, will have a new meaning to Wall Street.' This was interpreted as pointing to a terrific jump in Sugar to-morrow."

"The Street" knew that the news bureau that sent out this item was friendly to Barry Conant and the "System," and that it would print nothing displeasing to them. Therefore, this must be, a foreword of the coming harvest of the bulls and the slaughter of the bears.

Others than Ike Bloomstein remarked upon the fact that Bob Brownley had hung close to the Sugar-pole all day, but when the close had come and gone without his having anything to do with the Sugar skyrockets, he dropped out of his fellow-brokers' minds. Wall Street has no use for any but the "doer." The poet and the mooner would be no more secure from interruption in the centre of the Sahara than in Wall Street between ten and three o'clock. Some sage has said that the human mind, like the well-bucket, can carry only its fill. The Wall Street mind always has its fill of budding dollars. In consequence, there is never room for those other interests that enter the normal mind.

Friday, the 13th of November, drifted over Manhattan Island in a drear drizzle of marrow-chilling haze, which just missed being rain—one of those New York days that give a hesitating suicide renewed courage to cut the mortal coil. By ten o'clock it had settled down on the Stock Exchange and its surrounding infernos with a clamminess that damped the spirits of the most rampant bulls. No class in the world is so susceptible to atmospheric conditions as stock-gamblers. Many a stout-hearted one has been known to postpone the inauguration of a long-planned coup merely because the air filled his blood with the dank chill of superstition. Because of the expected Sugar pyrotechnics, Stock Exchange members had gathered early; the brokers' offices were crowded to overflowing before ten; the morning papers, not only in New York but in Boston, Philadelphia, and other centres, were filled with stories of the big rise that was to take place in Sugar. The knowing ones saw the ear-marks of the "System's" press-agent in these stories; and they knew that this industrious institution had not sat up the night before because of insomnia. All the signs pointed to a killing, and a terrific one—pointed so plainly that the bears and Sugar shorts found no hope in the atmosphere or the date.

Bob had not been near the office the afternoon before, and as he had not come in by five minutes to ten I decided to go over to the Exchange and see if he were going to mix up in the baiting of the Sugar bears. I had no specific reasons for thinking he was interested except his recent queer actions, particularly his hanging to the Sugar-pole, yet doing nothing, the day before. But it is one of the best-established traditions of stock-gambledom that when an operator has been bitten by a rabid stock he is invariably attracted to it every time afterward that it shows signs of frothing. More than all, I had one of those strong nowhere-born-nowhere-cradled intuitions common to those living in the stock-gambling world, which made me feel the creepy shadow of coming events.

As on that day a few weeks before, the crowd was at the Sugar-pole, but its alignment was different. There in the centre were Barry Conant and his trusted lieutenants, but no opposing rival. None of those hundreds of brokers showed that desperate resolve to do or die that is born of a necessity. They were there to buy or sell, but not to put up a life or death, on-me-depends-the-result fight. Those who were long of stock could easily be distinguished by their expressions of joy from the shorts, who had seen the handwriting on the wall and were filled with uncertainty, fear, terror. The demeanour of Barry Conant and his lieutenants expressed confidence: they were going to do what they were there to do. They showed by their tight-buttoned coats, and squared shoulders that they expected lots of rush, push, and haul work, but apparently they anticipated no last-ditch fighting. The gong pealed and the crowd of brokers sprang at one another, but only for blood, not flesh, bone, heart, and soul; just blood. The first price on Sugar was 211 for 3,000 shares. Someone sold it in a block. Barry Conant bought it. It did not require three eyes to see that the seller was one of his lieutenants. This meant what is known as a "wash" sale, a fictitious one arranged in advance between two brokers to establish the basis for the trades that are to follow—one of those minor frauds of stock-gambling by which the public is deceived and the traders and plungers are handicapped with loaded dice. In principle, it is a device older than stock exchanges themselves, and is put to use elsewhere than on the floor. For instance, four genuine buyers want a particular animal worth $200 at a horse auction. Its owner's pal starts the bidding at $400, and the four, not being up in horse values, are thereby induced to reach for it at between $400 to $500. But human nature, whether at horse sales or at stock-gambling, loves to be "hinky-dinked" as much as the moth loves to play tag with the candle flame. In five minutes Sugar was selling at 221, and the frantic shorts were grabbing for it as though there never was to be another share put on sale, while Barry Conant and his lieutenants were most industriously pushing it just beyond their reaching finger-tips, either by buying it as fast as it was offered by genuine sellers or by taking what their own pals threw in the air.

I was not surprised to see Bob's tall form wedged in the crowd about two-thirds of the way from the centre. Every other active floor member was there too. Even Ike Bloomstein and Joe Barnes, who seldom went into the big crowds, were on hand, perhaps to catch a flier for their Thanksgiving turkey money, perhaps to get as near the killing as possible. Bob was not trading, although, as on the day before, he never took his eye off Barry Conant. I said to myself, "He is trying to fathom Barry Conant's movements," but for what purpose puzzled me. The hands of the big clock on the wall showed that trading had been thirty minutes under way and still Barry Conant was pushing up the price. His voice had just rung out "25 for any part of 5,000" when, like an echo, sounded through the hall, "Sold." It was Bob. He had worked his way to the centre of the crowd and stood in front of Barry Conant. He was not the Bob who had taken Barry Conant's gaff that afternoon a few weeks before. I never saw him cooler, calmer, more self-possessed.

He was the incarnation of confident power. A cold, cynical smile played around the corners of his mouth as he looked down upon his opponent.

The effect upon Barry Conant was different from that of Bob's last bid on the day when Beulah Sands's hopes went skyward in dust. It did not rouse him to the wild, furious desire for the onslaught that he showed then, but seemed to quicken his alert, prolific mind to exercise all its cunning. I think that in that one moment Barry Conant recalled his suspicions of the day before, when he had wondered what Bob's presence in the crowd meant, and that he saw again the picture of Bob on the day when he himself had ditched Bob's treasure-train. He hesitated for just the fraction of a second, while he waved with lightning-like rapidity a set of finger signals to his lieutenants. Then he squared himself for the encounter. "25 for 5,000," Cold, cold as the voice of a condemning judge rang Bob's "Sold." "25 for 5,000." "Sold." "25 for 5,000." "Sold." Their eyes were fixed upon each other, in Barry's a defiant glare, in Bob's mingled pity and contempt. The rest of the brokers hushed their own bids and offers until it could have truthfully been said that the floor of the Stock Exchange was quiet, an almost unheard-of thing in like circumstances. Again Barry Conant's voice, "25 for 5,000." "Sold." "25 for 5,000." "Sold." Barry Conant had met his master. Whether it was that for the first time in all his wonderful career he realised that the "System" was to meet its Nemesis, or what the cause, none could tell, perhaps not even Barry Conant himself, but some emotion caused his olive face for an instant to turn pale, and gave his voice a tell-tale quiver. Once more pealed forth "25 for 5,000." That Bob saw the pallor, that he caught the quiver, was evident to all, for the instant his "Sold" rang out, he followed it with "5,000 at 24, 23, 22, 20." Neither Barry Conant nor any of his lieutenants got in a "Take it"; although whether they wanted to or not was an open question until Bob allowed his voice to dwell just a pendulum swing of time on the 20. It was as if he were tantalising them into sticking by their guns. By the time he paused, Barry Conant's nerve was back, for his piercing "Take it" had linked to it "20 for any part of 10,000." The bid was yet on his lips when Bob's deep voice rang out "Sold." "Any part of 25,000 at 19, 18, 15, 10." Hell was now loose. Back and forth, up against the rail, around the room and back and around again, the crowd surged for fifteen of the wildest, craziest minutes in the history of the New York Stock Exchange, a history replete with records of wild and crazy scenes.

At last from sheer exhaustion there came a ten minutes' lull, which was used in comparing trades. At the beginning of the respite Sugar was selling at 155, for in that quarter-hour of madness it had broken from 210 to 155, but when the ten minutes had elapsed, the stock had worked back to 167. Barry Conant had again taken the centre of the crowd after hastily scanning the brief notes handed him by messenger-boys and giving orders to his lieutenants. He had evidently received reinforcements in the form of renewed orders from his principals. Many of the faces that fringed the inner circle of that crowd were frightful to look upon, some white as though just lifted from hospital pillows, others red to the verge of apoplexy—all strained as though awaiting the coming of the jury with a life or death verdict. They all knew that Bob had sold more than a hundred thousand shares of Sugar upon which the profits must be more than four million dollars. Would he resume selling or was he through? Was it short stock, which must be bought back, or long stock; and if long, whose stock? Were the insiders selling out on one another, or were they all selling together, and under cover of Barry Conant's movements were Camemeyer and "Standard Oil" emptying their bag preparatory to the slaughter of the Washington contingent? All these questions were rushing through the heads of that crowd of brokers like steam through a boiler, now hot, now cold, but always at high pressure, for upon the correctness of the answers depended the fortune of many who breathlessly awaited the renewal or the suspension of the contest. Even Barry Conant's usually impassive face wore a tinge of anxiety.

Indeed, Bob's was the only one in the centre of that throng that showed no sign of what was going on behind it. The same cynical smile that had been there since the opening still played around the corners of his mouth as he squared himself in front of his opponent. All knew now that he was not through. Barry Conant had evidently decided to force the fighting, although more cautiously than before. "67 for a thousand." One of his lieutenants bid 67 for 500, another 67 for 300, and as Bob had not yet shown his intention of meeting their bids, 67 for different amounts was heard all over the crowd. Bob might have been tossing a mental coin to decide the advisability of buying back what he had sold; he might have been adding up the bids as they were made. He said nothing for a fraction of a minute, which to those tortured men must have seemed like an age. Then with a wave of his hand, as though delivering a benediction, he swept the circle with a cold-blooded, "Sold the lots. 5,600 in all."

"Sixty-seven for a thousand"—again Barry Conant's bid. "Sold." "67 for 5,000." "Sold." "66 for a thousand." "Sold." The drop from five thousand to one thousand and a dollar a share in Barry Conant's bids was the mortally wounded but still game general's "Sound the retreat." Bob heard it. "Any part of 10,000 at 65, 64, 62, 60." The din was now as fierce as before. The entire crowd, all but Barry Conant and his lieutenants, seemed to have concluded that Bob's renewal of attack meant that his was the winning side, and those who had been hanging on to their stock, hoping against hope, and those who were short and had been undecided whether to cover or to hold on and sell more for greater profits, vied with one another in a frantic effort to sell. All could now feel the coming panic. All could see that it was to be a bad one, as the least informed on the floor knew that there was a tremendous amount of Sugar stock in the hands of Washington novices at speculation and of others who had bought it at high prices. Sugar was now dropping two, three, five dollars a share between trades, and the panic was spreading to the other poles, as is always the case, for when there are sudden large losses in one stock, the losers must throw over the other stocks they hold to meet this loss, and thus the whole structure tumbles like a house of cards. Sugar had just crossed 110 when the loud bang of the president's gavel resounded through the room. Instantly there was a silence as of death. All knew the meaning of the sound, the most ominous ever heard in a stock exchange, calling for the temporary suspension of business while the president announces the failure of some member or house.

Perkins, Blanchard & Company

Announce that They Cannot Meet Their Obligations

This statement that one of the oldest houses had been swamped in the crash Bob had started caused further frantic selling, and, as though every member had employed the lull to refill his lungs, a howl arose that pealed and wailed to the dome.

I watched Bob closely; in fact, it was impossible for me to take my eyes off him; he seemed absolutely unmindful of the agonised shrieks about him, for the frenzied brokers were no longer crying their bids or offers, but screaming them. He still continued relentlessly to hammer Sugar, offering it in thousand and tens of thousand lots.

Again and again the gavel fell, and again and again an announcement of failure was followed by blood-curdling howls. When Sugar struck 80—not 180, but plain 80—it seemed that the last day of stock speculation was at hand. Announcements were being made every few minutes of the failure of this bank, the closing of the doors of that trust company. Where would it end? What power could stop this Niagara of molten dollars? Suddenly above the tumult rose Bob Brownley's voice. He must have been standing on his tiptoes. His hands were raised aloft. He seemed to tower a head above the mob. His voice was still clear and unimpaired by the terrible strain of the past two hours. To that mob it must have sounded like the trumpet of the delivering angel. "80 for any part of 25,000 Sugar." Instantly Sugar was hurled at him from all sides of the crowd. He was the only buyer of moment who had appeared since Sugar broke 125. Barry Conant and his lieutenants had disappeared like snowflakes at the opening of the door of the firebox of a locomotive speeding through the storm. In a few seconds Bob had been sold all the 25,000 he had bid for. Again his voice rang out: "80 for 25,000." The sellers momentarily halted. He got only a few thousands of his twenty-five. "85 for 25,000." A few thousands more. "90 for 25,000." Still fewer thousands. His bidding was beginning to tell on the mob. A cry ran through the room into the crowds around the other poles—"Brownley has turned!"—and taking renewed courage at the report, the bulls rallied their forces and began to bid for the different stocks, which a moment before it had seemed that no one wanted at any price.

In a chip of a minute the whole scene changed; there was almost as wild a panic on the up side as there had been on the down. Bob Brownley continued buying Sugar until he had pushed it above 150. He then went about tallying up his trades. At the end of ten minutes' calculation he returned to the centre and bought 11,000 shares more; coming out, his eye caught mine.

"Jim, have you been here long?"

"An eternity. I was here at the opening and I pray God never to put me through another two hours like the past two. It seems a hideous dream, a nightmare. Bob, in the name of God what have you been doing?"

He gave me a wild, awful look of exultation. Sublime triumph shone in those blazing brown orbs, triumph such as I had never seen in the eyes of man.

"Jim Randolph, I have been giving Wall Street and its hell 'System' a dose of its own poison, a good full-measure dose. They planned by harvesting a fresh crop of human hearts and souls on the bull side to give Friday the 13th a new meaning. Tradition says Friday the 13th is bear Saints' day. I believe in maintaining old traditions, so I harvested their hearts instead. I will tell you about it some time, Jim, but now I must see Beulah Sands. Jim Randolph, I've saved her and her father. I've made them a round three millions and a strong seven millions for myself."

He almost yelled it as he rushed away and left me dazed, stupefied. A moment, and I came to. Something urged me to follow him.

Chapter VI

AS I PASSED through my office a few minutes later I heard Bob's voice in Beulah Sands's office. It was raised in passionate eloquence.

"Yes, Beulah, I have done it single-handed. I have crucified Camemeyer, 'Standard Oil,' and the 'System' that spiked me to the cross a few weeks ago. You have three millions, and I have seven. Now there is nothing more but for you to go home to your father, and then come back to me. Back to me, Beulah, back to me to be my wife!"

He stopped. There was no sound. I waited; then, frightened, I stepped to the door of Beulah Sands's office. Bob was standing just inside the threshold, where he had halted to give her the glad tidings. She had risen from her desk and was looking at him with an agonised stare. He seemed to be transfixed by her look, the wild ecstasy of the outburst of love yet mirrored in his eyes. She was just saying as I reached the door:

"Bob, in mercy's name tell me you got this money fairly, honourably."

Bob must have realised for the first time what he had done. He did not speak. He only stared into her eyes. She was now at his side.

"Bob, you are unnerved," she said; "you have been through a terrible ordeal. For an hour I have been reading in the bulletins of the banks and trust companies that have failed, of the banking-houses that have been ruined. I have been reading that you did it; that you have made millions—and I knew it was for me, for father, but in the midst of my joy, my gratitude, my love—for, oh, Bob, I love you," she interrupted herself passionately; "it seems as though I love you beyond the capacity of a human heart to love. I think that for the right to be yours for one single moment of this life I would smilingly endure all the pains and miseries of eternal torture. Yes, Bob, for the right to have you call me yours for only while I heard the word, I would do anything, Bob, anything that was honourable."

She had drawn his head down close to her face, and her great blue eyes searched his as though they would go to his very soul. She was a child in her simple appeal for him to allow her to see his heart, to see that there was nothing black there.

As she gazed, her beautiful hands played through his hair as do a mother's through that of the child she is soothing in sickness.

"Bob, speak to me, speak to me," she begged, "tell me there was no dishonour in the getting of those millions. Tell me no one was made to suffer as my father and I have suffered. Tell me that the suicides and the convicts, the daughters dragged to shame and the mothers driven to the madhouse as a result of this panic, cannot be charged to anything unfair or dishonourable that you have done. Bob, oh, Bob, answer! Answer no, or my heart will break; or if, Bob, you have made a mistake, if you have done that which in your great desire to aid me and my father seemed justifiable, but which you now see was wrong, tell it to me, Bob dear, and together we will try to undo it. We will try to find a way to atone. We will give the millions to the last, last penny to those upon whom you have brought misery. Father's loss will not matter. Together we will go to him and tell him what we have done, what we have lived through, tell him of our mistake, and in our agony he will forget his own. For such a horror has my father of anything dishonourable that he will embrace his misery as happiness when he knows that his teachings have enabled his daughter to undo this great wrong. And then, Bob, we will be married, and you and I and father and mother will be together, and be, oh, so happy, and we will begin all over again."

"Beulah, stop; in the name of God, in the name of your love for me, don't say another word. There is a limit to the capacity of a man to suffer, even if he be a great, strong brute like myself, and, Beulah, I have reached that limit. The day has been a hard one."

His voice softened and became as a tired child's.

"I must go out into the hustle of the street, into the din and sound, and get down my nerves and get back my head. Then I shall be able to think clear and true, and I will come back to you, and together we will see if I have done anything that makes me unfit to touch the cheek and the hands and the lips of the best and most beautiful woman God ever put upon earth. Beulah, you know I would not deceive you to save my body from the fires of this world, and my soul from the torture of the damned, and I promise you that if I find that I have done wrong, what you call wrong, what your father would call wrong, I will do what you say to atone."

He took her head between his hands, gently, reverently, and touching his lips to her glorious golden hair, he went away.

Beulah Sands turned to me. "Please, Mr. Randolph, go with him. He is soul-dazed. One can never tell what a heart sorely perplexed will prompt its owner to do. Often in the night when I have got myself into a fever from thinking of my father's situation, I have had awful temptations. The agents of the devil seek the wretched when none of those they love are by. I have often thought some of the blackest tragedies of the earth might have been averted if there had been a true friend to stand at the wrung one's elbow at the fatal minute of decision and point to the sun behind, just when the black ahead grew unendurable. Please follow Mr. Brownley that you may be ready, should his awakening to what he has done become unbearable. Tell him the dreaded morrows are never as terrible actually as they seem in anticipation."

I overtook Bob just outside the office. I did not speak to him, for I realised that he was in no mood for company. I dropped in behind, determined that I would not lose sight of him. It was almost one o'clock. Wall Street was at its meridian of frenzy, every one on a wild rush. The day's doing had packed the always-crowded money lane. The newsboys were shouting afternoon editions. "Terrible panic in Wall Street. One man against millions. Robert Brownley broke 'the Street.' Made twenty millions in an hour. Banks failed. Wreck and ruin everywhere. President Snow of Asterfield National a suicide." Bob gave no sign of hearing. He strode with a slow, measured gait, his head erect, his eyes staring ahead at space, a man thinking, thinking, thinking for his salvation. Many hurrying men looked at him, some with an expression of unutterable hatred, as though they wanted to attack him. Then again there were those who called him by name with a laugh of joy; and some turned to watch him in curiosity. It was easy to pick the wounded from those who shared in his victory, and from those who knew the frenzied finance buzz-saw only by its buzz. Bob saw none. Where could he be going? He came to the head of the street of coin and crime and crossed Broadway. His path was blocked by the fence surrounding old Trinity's churchyard. Grasping the pickets in either hand he stared at the crumbling headstones of those guardsmen of Mammon who once walked the earth and fought their heart battles, as he was walking and fighting, but who now knew no ten o'clock, no three, who looked upon the stock-gamblers and dollar-trailers as they looked upon the worms that honeycombed their headstones' bases. What thoughts went through Bob Brownley's mind only his Maker knew. For minutes he stood motionless, then he walked on down Broadway. He went into the Battery. The benches were crowded with that jetsam and flotsam of humanity that New York's mighty sewers throw in armies upon her inland beaches at every sunrise: Here a sodden brute sleeping off a prolonged debauch, there a lad whose frankness of face and homespun clothes and bewildered eyes spelt, "from the farm and mother's watchful love." On another bench an Italian woman who had a half-dozen future dollar kings and social queens about her, and whose clothes told of the immigrant ship just into port. Bob Brownley apparently saw none. But suddenly he stopped. Upon a bench sat a sweet-faced mother holding a sleeping babe in her arms, while a curly-pated boy nestled his head in her lap and slept through the magic lanes and fairy woods of dreamland. The woman's face was one of those that blend the confidence of girlhood with the uncertainty of womanhood. 'Twas a pretty face, which had been plainly tagged by its Maker for a light-hearted trip through this world, but it had been seared by the iron of the city.

"Mr. Brownley—" She started to rise.

He gently pushed her back with a "hush," unwilling to rob the sleepers of their heaven.

"What are you doing here, Mrs.——?" He halted.

"Mrs. Chase. Mr. Brownley, when I went away from Randolph & Randolph's office I married John Chase; you may remember him as delivery clerk. I had such a happy home and my husband was so good; I did not have to typewrite any longer. These are our two children."

"What are you doing here?"

The tears sprang to her eyes; she dropped them, but did not answer.

"Don't mind me, woman. I, too, have hidden hells I don't want the world to see. Don't mind me; tell me your story. It may do you good; it may do me good; yes, it may do me good."

I had dropped into a seat a few feet away. Both were too much occupied with their own thoughts to notice me or any one else. I could not overhear their conversation, but long afterward, when I mentioned our old stenographer, Bessie Brown, to Bob, he told me of the incident at the Battery. Her husband, after their marriage, had become infected with the stock-gambling microbe, the microbe that gnaws into its victim's mind and heart day and night, while ever fiercer grows the "get rich, get rich" fever. He had plunged with their savings and had drawn a blank. He had lost his position in disgrace and had landed in the bucket-shop, the sub-cellar pit of the big Stock Exchange hell. From there a week before he had been sent to prison for theft, and that morning she had been turned into the street by her landlord. I saw Bob take from his pocket his memorandum-book, write something upon a leaf, tear it out and hand it to the woman, touch his hat, and before she could stop him, stride away. I saw her look at the paper, clap her hands to her forehead, look at the paper again and at the retreating form of Bob Brownley. Then I saw her, yes, there in the old Battery Park, in the drizzling rain and under the eyes of all, drop upon her knees in prayer. How long she prayed I do not know. I only know that as I followed Bob I looked back and the woman was still upon her knees. I thought at the time how queer and unnatural the whole thing seemed. Later, I learned to know that nothing is queer and unnatural in the world of human suffering; that great human suffering turns all that is queer and unnatural into commonplace. Next day Bessie Brown came to our office to see Bob. Not being able to get at him she asked for me.

"Mr. Randolph, tell me, please, what shall I do with this paper?" she said. "I met Mr. Brownley in the Battery yesterday. He saw I was in distress and he gave me this, but I cannot believe he meant it," and she showed me an order on Randolph & Randolph for a thousand dollars. I cashed her check and she went away.

From the Battery Bob sought the wharves, the Bowery, Five Points, the hothouses of the under-worldlings of America. He seemed bent on picking out the haunts of misery in the misery-infested metropolis of the new world. For two hours he tramped and I followed. A number of times I thought to speak to him and try to win him from his mood, but I refrained. I could see there was a soul battle waging and I realised that upon its outcome might depend Bob's salvation. Some seek the quiet of the woods, the soothing rustle of the leaves, the peaceful ripple of the brook when battling for their soul, but Bob's woods appeared to be the shadowy places of misery, his rustling leaves the hoarse din of the multitude, and his brook's ripple the tears and tales of the man-damned of the great city, for he stopped and conversed with many human derelicts that he met on his course. The hand of the clock on Trinity's steeple pointed to four as we again approached the office of Randolph & Randolph. Bob was now moving with a long, hurried stride, as though consumed with a fever of desire to get to Beulah Sands. For the last fifteen minutes I had with difficulty kept him in sight. Had he arrived at a decision, and if so, what was it? I asked myself over and over again as I plowed through the crowds.

Bob went straight to Beulah Sands's office, I to mine. I had been there but a moment when I heard deep, guttural groans. I listened. The sound came louder than before. It came from Beulah Sands's office. With a bound I was at the open door. My God, the sight that met my gaze! It haunts me even now when years have dulled its vividness. The beautiful, quiet, gray figure that had grown to be such a familiar picture to Bob and me of late, sat at the flat desk in the centre of the room. She faced the door. Her elbows rested on the desk; in her hand was an afternoon paper that she had evidently been reading when Bob entered. God knows how long she had been reading it before he came. Bob was kneeling at the side of her chair, his hands clasped and uplifted in an agony of appeal that was supplemented by the awful groans. His face showed unspeakable terror and entreaty; the eyes were bursting from their sockets and were riveted on hers as those of a man in a dungeon might be fixed upon an approaching spectre of one whom he had murdered. His chest rose and fell, as though trying to burst some unseen bonds that were crushing out his life. With every breath would come the awful groan that had first brought me to him. Beulah Sands had half turned her face until her eyes gazed into Bob's with a sweet, childish perplexity. I looked at her, surprised that one whom I had always seen so intelligently masterful should be passive in the face of such anguish. Then, horror of horrors! I saw that there was something missing from her great blue eyes. I looked; gasped. Could it possibly be? With a bound I was at her side. I gazed again into those eyes which that morning had been all that was intelligent, all that was godlike, all that was human. Their soul, their life was gone. Beulah Sands was a dead woman; not dead in body, but in soul; the magic spark had fled. She was but an empty shell—a woman of living flesh and blood; but the citadel of life was empty, the mind was gone. What had been a woman was but a child. I passed my hand across my now damp forehead. I closed my eyes and opened them again. Bob's figure, with clasped, uplifted hands, and bursting eyes, was still there. There still resounded through the room the awful guttural groans. Beulah Sands smiled, the smile of an infant in the cradle. She took one beautiful hand from the paper and passed it over Bob's bronzed cheek, just as the infant touches its mother's face with its chubby fingers. In my horror I almost expected to hear the purling of a babe. My eyes in their perplexity must have wandered from her face, for I suddenly became aware of a great black head-line spread across the top of the paper that she had been reading:

"FRIDAY, THE 13TH."

And beneath in one of the columns:

"TERRIBLE TRAGEDY IN VIRGINIA"

"THE MOST PROMINENT CITIZEN OF THE STATE, EX-UNITED STATES SENATOR AND EX-GOVERNOR, JUDGE LEE SANDS OF SANDS LANDING, WHILE TEMPORARILY INSANE FROM THE LOSS OF HIS

FORTUNE AND MILLIONS OF THE FUNDS FOR WHICH HE WAS TRUSTEE, CUT THE THROAT OF HIS INVALID WIFE, HIS DAUGHTER'S, AND THEN HIS OWN. ALL THREE DIED INSTANTLY."

In another column:

"ROBERT BROWNLEY CREATES THE MOST DISASTROUS PANIC IN THE HISTORY OF WALL STREET AND SPREADS WRECK AND RUIN THROUGHOUT THE COUNTRY."

A hideous picture seared its every light and shade on my mind, through my heart, into all my soul. A frenzied-finance harvest scene with its gory crop; in the centre one living-dead, part of the picture, yet the ghost left to haunt the painters, one of whom was already cowering before the black and bloody canvas.

Well did the word-artist who wrote over the door of the madhouse, "Man can suffer only to the limit, then he shall know peace," understand the wondrous wisdom of his God. Beulah Sands had gone beyond her limit and was at peace.

The awful groaning stopped and an ashen pallor spread over Bob Brownley's face. Before I could catch him he rolled backward upon the floor as dead. Bob Brownley, too, had gone beyond his limit. I bent over him and lifted his head, while the sweet woman-child knelt and covered his face with kisses, calling in a voice like that of a tiny girl speaking to her doll, "Bob, my Bob, wake up, wake up; your Beulah wants you." As I placed my hand upon Bob's heart and felt its beats grow stronger, as I listened to Beulah Sands's childish voice, joyously confident, as it called upon the one thing left of her old world, some of my terror passed. In its place came a great mellowing sense of God's marvellous wisdom. I thought gratefully of my mother's always ready argument that the law of all laws, of God and nature, is that of compensation. I had allowed Bob's head to sink until it rested in Beulah's lap, and from his calm and steady breathing I could see that he had safely passed a crisis, that at least he was not in the clutches of death, as I had at first feared.

Bob slept. Beulah Sands ceased her calling and with a smile raised her fingers to her lips and softly said, "Hush, my Bob's asleep." Together we held vigil over our sleeping lover and friend, she with the happiness of a child who had no fear of the awakening, I with a silent terror of what should come next. I had seen one mind wafted to the unknown that day. Was it to have a companion to cheer and solace it on its far journey to the great beyond? How long we waited Bob's awakening I could not tell. The clock's hands said an hour; it seemed to me an age. At last his magnificent physique, his unpoisoned blood and splendid brain pulled him through to his new world of mind and heart torture. His eyelids lifted. He looked at me, then at Beulah Sands, with eyes so sad, so awful in their perplexed mournfulness, that I almost wished they had never opened, or had opened to let me see the childlike look that now shone from the girl's. His gaze finally rested on her and his lips murmured "Beulah."

"There, Bob, I thought you would know it was time to wake up." She bent over and kissed him on the eyes again and again with the loving ardour a child bestows upon its pets.

He slowly rose to his feet. I could see from his eyes and the shudder that went over him as he caught sight of the paper on the desk that he was himself; that memory of the happenings of the day had not fled in his sleep. He rose to his full height, his head went up, and his shoulders back, but only from habit and for an instant. Then he folded Beulah Sands to his breast and dropped his head upon her shoulder. He sobbed like a father with the corpse of his child.

"Why, Bob, my Bob, is this the way you treat your Beulah when she's let you sleep so your beautiful eyes would be pretty for the wedding? Is this the way to act before this kind man who has come to take us to the church? Naughty, naughty Bob."

I looked at her, at Bob, in horror. I was beginning to realise the absolute deadness of this woman. From the first look I had known that her mind had fled, but knowledge is not always realisation. She did not even know who I was. Her mind was dead to all but the man she loved, the man who through all those long days of her suffering she had silently worshiped. To all but him she was new-born.

At the sound of "wedding," "church," Bob's head slowly rose from her shoulder. I saw his decision the instant I caught his eye; I realised the uselessness of opposing it, and, sick at heart and horrified, I listened as he said in a voice now calm and soothing as that of a father to his child, "Yes, Beulah, my darling, I have slept too long. Bob has been naughty, but we will make up for lost time. Get your hat and cloak and we'll hurry to the church or we will be late."

With a laugh of joy she followed him to the closet where hung the little gray turban and the pretty gray jacket. He took them from their peg and gave them to her.

"Not a word, Jim," he bade me. "In the name of God and all our friendship, not a word. Beulah Sands will be my wife as soon as I can find a minister to marry us. It is best, best. It is right. It is as God would have it, or I am not capable of knowing right from wrong. Anyway, it is what will be. She has no father, no mother, no sister, no one to protect and shield her. The 'System' has robbed her of all in life, even of herself, of everything, Jim, but me. I must try to win her back for herself, or to make her new world a happy one—a happy one for her."

Chapter VII

AN OLD GAMBLER, whose life had been spent listening to the rattle of the drop-in-bound-out little roulette ball, was told by a fellow victim, as his last dollar went to the relentless tiger's maw, that the keeper's foot was upon an electric button which enabled him to make the ball drop where his stake was not. He simply said, "Thank God. I thought that prince of cheats, Fate, who all through life has had his foot on the button of my game, was the one who did the trick." Long suffering had driven the old gambler to the loser's bible, Philosophy! Cheated by man's device, he knew he had some chance of getting even; but Fate he could not combat.

Bob Brownley had thought himself in hard luck when his eyes opened to the fact that he had been robbed by means of dice loaded by man, but when Fate pressed the button he saw that his man-made hell was but a feeble imitation, and—was satisfied, as whoever knows the game of life is satisfied, because—he must be. Bob's strong head bowed, his iron will bent, and meekly his soul murmured, "Thy will be done."

That night he married Beulah Sands. The minister who united the grown-up man and the woman who was as a new-born babe saw nothing extraordinary in the match. He murmured to me, who acted as best man to the groom, maid of honour to the bride, and father and mother to both, "We see strange sights, we ministers of the great city, Mr. Randolph. The sweet little lady appears to be a trifle scared." My explanation that she and Mr. Brownley were the only survivors of the awful tragedies of the day was sufficient. He was satisfied when he got no other response to his question, "Do you take this man to be your wedded husband?" than a sweet childish smile as she snuggled closer to Bob.

Bob and his bride went South to his mother and sisters the next day. He left to me the settlement of his trades. He instructed me to set aside $3,000,000 profits for Beulah Sands-Brownley, and insisted that I pay from the balance the notes he had given me a few weeks before. There remained something over $5,000,000 for himself.

The leading Wall Street paper, in its preachment on the panic, wound up with:

> "Wall Street has lived through many black Fridays. Some of them have been thirteenth-of-the-month Fridays, but no Friday yet marked from the calendar, no Saturday, Monday, Tuesday, Wednesday, or Thursday yet garnered to the storehouse of the past was ever more jubilantly welcomed by his Satanic Majesty than yesterday. We pray heaven no coming day may be ordained to go against yesterday's record for tigerish cruelty and awful destruction. It is rumoured that Mr. Brownley of Randolph & Randolph, either for himself or his clients cleared twenty-five millions of profit. We believe that this estimate is low. The losses coming through Robert Brownley's terrible onslaught must have run over five hundred millions. Wall Street and the country will do well to take the moral of yesterday's market to their heart. It is this: The concentration of wealth in the hands of a few Americans is a menace to our financial structure. It is the unanimous opinion of 'the Street' that Robert Brownley could never have succeeded in battering down the price of Sugar in the very teeth of the Camemeyer and Standard Oil support as he did yesterday, without a cash backing of from fifty to one hundred millions. If a vast aggregation of money owners deliberately place themselves behind an onslaught such as was so successfully made yesterday, why can that

slaughter not be repeated at any time, on any stock, and against the support of any backing?"

When I read this and listened to talk along the same lines, I was puzzled. I could not for the life of me see where Bob Brownley could have got five to ten millions' backing for such a raid, much less fifty to a hundred. Yet I was forced to confess that he must have had some tremendous backing; else how could he have done what I had seen him do?

Bob left his wife at his mother's house while he went to Sands Landing to the funeral. After the old judge and his victims had been laid away and the relatives had gathered in the library of the great white Sands mansion, he explained their kinswoman's condition and told them that she was his wife. He insisted upon paying all Judge Sands's debts, over $500,000 of which was owed to members of the Sands family for whom he had been trustee. Before he went back to his mother's, Bob had turned a great calamity into an occasion for something near rejoicing. Judge Sands and his family were very dear to the people of the section, but his misfortune had threatened such wide-spread ruin that the unlooked-for recovery of a million and a half was a godsend that made for happiness.

Two days after the funeral Bob's dearest hope fled. He had ordered all things at the Sands plantation put in their every-day condition. Beulah Sands's uncles, aunts, and cousins had arranged to welcome her and to try by every means in their power to coax back her lost mind. They assured Bob that, barring the absence of Beulah's father, mother, and sister, there would not be a memory-recaller missing. Bob and his wife landed from the river packet at the foot of the driveway, which led straight from the landing to the vine-covered, white-pillared portico. Bob's agony must have been awful when his wife clapped her hands in childish joy as she exclaimed, "Oh, Bob, what a pretty place!" She gave no sign that she had ever seen the great entrance, through which she had come and gone from her babyhood. Bob took her to the library, to her mother's room, to her own, to the nursery where were the dolls and toys of her childhood, but there came no sign of recognition, nothing but childish pleasure. She looked at her aunts and uncles and the cousins with whom she had spent her life, bewildered at finding so many strangers in the otherwise quiet place. As a last hope, they led in her old black foster-mother, who had nursed her in babyhood, who was the companion of her childhood and the pet of her womanhood. There was not a dry eye in the library when she met the old mammy's outburst of joy with the puzzled gaze of the child who does not understand. The grief of the old negress was pitiful as she realised that she was a stranger to her "honey bird." The child seemed perplexed at her grief. It was plain to all that the Sands home meant nothing to the last of the judge's family.

Bob brought her back to New York and besought the aid of the medical experts of America and of the Old World to regain that which had been recalled by its Maker. The doctors were fascinated with this new phase of mind blight, for in some particulars Beulah's case was unlike any known instances, but none gave hope. All agreed that some wire connecting heart and brain had burned out when the cruel "System" threw on a voltage beyond the wire's capacity to transmit. All agreed that the woman-child wife would never grow older unless through some mental eruption beyond human power to produce. Some of the medical men pointed to one possibility, but that one was too terrible for Bob to entertain.

The first anniversary of their marriage found Bob and his wife settled in their new Fifth Avenue mansion. He had bought and torn down two old houses between Forty-second and Forty-third Streets and had erected a palace, the inside of which was unique among all New York's unusual structures. The first and second floors were all that refined taste and unlimited expenditure of money could produce. Nothing on those splendid floors told of the strange things above. A sedate luxury pervaded the drawing-rooms, library, and dining-room. Bob said to me, in taking me through them, "Some day, Jim, Beulah may recover, may come back to me, and I want to have everything as she would wish, everything as she would have had it if the curse had never come." The third floor was Beulah's. A child's dainty bedroom; two nurses' rooms adjoining; a nursery, with a child's small schoolroom and a big playroom, with dolls and doll houses, child's toys of every description in abandon, as though their owner were in fact but a few years old. Across the hall were three offices, exact duplicates of mine, Bob's, and Beulah Sands's at Randolph & Randolph's. When I first saw them it was with difficulty that I brought myself to realise that I was not where the gruesome happenings of a year before had taken place. Bob had reproduced to the minutest details our down-town workshop. Standing in the door of Beulah Sands's office I faced the flat desk at which she had sat the afternoon when I first saw that hideous result of the work of the "System." I could almost see the little gray figure holding the afternoon paper. In horror my eyes sought the floor at the side of the chair in search of Bob's agonised face and uplifted hands. As I stood for the first time in the middle of Bob's handiwork, I seemed to hear again those awful groans.

"Jim," Bob said, "I have a haunting idea that some day Beulah will wake and look around and think she has been but a few minutes asleep. If she should, she must have nothing to disabuse her mind until we break the news to her. I have instructed her nurses, one or the other of whom never loses sight of her night or day, to win her to the habit of spending her time at her old desk; I have told them always to be prepared for her awakening, and when it comes they are instantly to shut off the rest of the floor and house until I can get to her. Here comes Beulah now."

Out of the nursery came a laughing, happy child-woman. In spite of her finely developed, womanly figure, which had lost nothing of its wonderful beauty, and the exquisite face and golden-brown hair and great blue eyes, which were as fascinating as on the day she first entered the offices of Randolph & Randolph; in spite of the close-fitting gray gown with dainty turned-over lace collar, I could hardly bring myself to believe that she was anything but a young child. With an eager look and a happy laugh she went to Bob and throwing her arms about his neck, covered his face with kisses.

"Good Bob has come back to play with Beulah," she said, "She knew he would. They told Beulah Bob had gone away to the woods to gather pretty flowers. Beulah knew if Bob had gone to the woods he would have taken Beulah with him. Now Bob must play school with Beulah." She sat at her desk and opened her child's school-book. With mock severity she said, "Bob, c-a-t. What does it spell?" For half an hour Bob sat and played scholar and teacher by turns with all the patience of a fond father. With difficulty I kept back the tears the sad sight brought to my eyes.

For the first year of Bob's marriage we saw but little of him at the office. The Exchange saw less. He had wandered in upon the floor two or three times, but did no business and seemed to take but little interest.

"The Street" knew Bob had married the daughter of Judge Lee Sands, the victim of Tom Reinhart's cold-blooded Seaboard Air Line deal. Otherwise it knew nothing of the affair. His friends never met his wife. Occasionally they would pass the Brownley carriage on the avenue or in the park and, taking it for granted that the beautiful woman was Mrs. Brownley, they thought Bob a lucky fellow. It seemed quite natural that his wife should choose seclusion after the awful tragedy at her home in Virginia. But they could not understand why, with such cause for mourning, the exquisite figure beside Bob in the victoria should always be garbed in gray. After a while it was whispered that there was something wrong in Bob's household. Then his friends and acquaintances ceased to whisper or to think of his affairs. With all New York's bad points—and they are as plentiful as her church spires and charity bazaars—she has one offsetting virtue. If a dweller in her midst chooses to let New York alone, New York is willing to reciprocate. In her most crowded fashionable districts a person may come and go for a lifetime, and none in the block in which he dwells will know when his coming and going ceases. When a New Yorker reads in his newspaper of the man who lives next door to him, "murdered and his body discovered by the gas man" or the tax collector, the butcher or the baker, as the case may be, he never thinks he may have been remiss in his neighbourly duties. There is no such word as "neighbour" in the New York City dictionary. It may have been there once, but, if so, it was long ago used as a stake for the barbed-wire fence of exclusive keep-your-distance-we-keep-our-distance-until-we-know-youness. It is told of a minister from the rural districts, an old-fashioned American, who came to New York to take charge of a parish, that he started out to make his calls and was seized in the hall of what in civilisation would have been his next-door neighbour. He was rushed away to Bellevue for examination as to sanity. The verdict was: "Insane. Had no letter of introduction and was not in the set."

Shortly after the first anniversary of his wedding Bob gave up his office with Randolph & Randolph and opened one for himself. He explained that he was giving up his commission business to devote all his time to personal trading. With the opening of his new office he again became the most active man on the floor. His trading was intermittent. For weeks he would not be seen at the Exchange or on "the Street." Then he would return and, after executing a series of brilliant trades, which were invariably successful, he would again disappear. He soon became known as the luckiest operator in Wall Street, and the beginning of his every new deal was the signal for his fast-growing following to tag on.

From time to time I learned that Beulah Sands was making no real improvement, though in some details she had learned as a child learns. But there was no indication that she would ever regain her lost mind.

Strange stories of Bob's doings began to seep into my office. For long periods he would disappear. Neither the nurses in charge of his wife, nor his brother, mother, and sisters, for whom he had purchased a mansion a few blocks above his own, would hear a word from him. Then he would return as suddenly as he had disappeared, and his wild eyes and haggard face would tell of a prolonged and desperate soul struggle. He drank often now, a habit he had never before indulged in.

For ten days before the second anniversary of his marriage he had been missing. On the morning of the anniversary he appeared at the Exchange, wild-eyed and dare-devil reckless. The market had been advancing for weeks and was at a high level. Tom Reinhart and his branch of the "System" were working out a new fleecing of the public in Union and Northern Pacific. At the strike of the gong Bob took possession of the Union Pacific pole and in thirty minutes had precipitated a panic by his merciless selling. Our house was heavily interested in the Pacifics, although not in connection with Reinhart and his crowd. As soon as I got word that Bob was the cause of the slaughter, I rushed over to the Exchange and working my way into the crowd, I begged a word with him. He had broken both stocks over fifty points a share and the panic was raging through the room. He glared at me, but finally followed me out into the lobby. At first he would not heed my appeal, but finally he said, "Jim, it is too bad to let up. I had determined to rub this devilish institution off the map, but if it really is a case of injury to the house, it's my opportunity to do something for you who have done so much for me, so here goes." He threw himself into the Union Pacific crowd, first giving an order to a group of his brokers, who jumped for a number of other poles. Almost instantly the panic was stayed and stocks were bounding upward two to five points at a leap. Bob continued buying Union Pacific and his brokers other stocks in unlimited quantities. Nothing like such a quick turn of the market had been seen before. His power to absorb stocks seemed to be boundless. It was estimated that personally and through his brokers he bought over half a million shares before he joined me and left the Exchange.

I looked at him in wonderment. "Bob, I cannot understand you," I said at last as we turned out of Broad Street into Wall. "It seems as if you work with magic. Everything you touch turns to gold."

He wheeled on me. "Yes, Jim, you are right. Gold, heartless, soulless gold. But what is the dross good for? What is it good for to me? To-day I suppose I have made the biggest one-man killing in the history of 'the Street.' I must be an easy twenty-five millions richer in gold than I was this morning, and I had enough then to dam the East River and a good section of the North. But tell me, Jim, tell me, what can it buy in this world that I have not got? I had health and happiness, perfect health, pure happiness, when I did not have a thousand all told. Now I have fifty millions, and I know how to get fifty or five hundred and fifty more any time I care to take them, and I have only physical and mental hell. No beggar in all the world is so poor in happiness as I. Tell me, tell me, Jim, in the name of God, if there is one—for already the game of gold is robbing me of my faith in God—where can I buy a little, just a little happiness with all this cursed yellow dirt? What will it get me in the next world, Jim Randolph, what will it get me? If I had died when I was poor, I think you will agree with me that, if there is a heaven, I should have stood an even chance of getting there. Now on a day like to-day, when you see the results of my work, the results of my handling of unlimited gold, you must agree that if I were taken off I should stand more than an even show of landing in hell where the sulphur is thickest and the flames are hottest."

We were at the entrance of Randolph & Randolph's office as he poured out this terrible torrent of bitterness. He glared at me as a dungeon prisoner might glare at his keeper for his answer to "Where can I find liberty?" I had no words to answer him. As I noted the awful changes his new life was making in every line of his face, the rigid hardness, the haunted, nervous look of desperation, which seemed a forerunner of madness, I could not see, either, where his millions brought any happiness. His hair, which once was smooth and orderly, hung over his forehead in an unparted mass of tangled curls, and here and there showed a streak of white. Bob Brownley was still handsome, even more fascinating than before the mercury entered his soul, but it was that wild, awful beauty of the caged lion, lashing himself into madness with memories of his lost freedom.

"Jim," he went on, when he saw I could not answer, "I guess you don't know where I can swap the yellow mud for balm of Gilead. I won't bother you with my troubles any longer. I will go up-town and see the little girl whose happiness Tom Reinhart needed in his business. I will go up and show her the pictures in this week's *Collier's* of the fine hospital for incurables that Reinhart has so generously and nobly built at a cost of two and a half millions! The little girl may think better of Reinhart when she knows that her father's money was put to such good use. Who knows but the great finance king may dedicate it as the 'Judge Lee Sands Home' and carve over the entrance a bas-relief of her father, mother, and sister with Hope, Faith, and Charity coming from the mouths of their hanging severed heads?"

Bob Brownley laughed a horrible ringing laugh as he uttered these awful words. Then he beat his hand down on my shoulders as he said in a hoarse voice, "Jim, but for you I should have had crimps in that jackal philanthropist's soul by now and in the souls of his kind. But never mind. He will keep; he will surely keep until I get to him. Every day he lives he will be fitter for the crimping. Within the short two years since he finished grilling Judge Sands's soul, he has put himself in better form to appreciate his reward. I see by the press that at last his aristocratic wife has gold-cured Newport of its habit of dating back the name Reinhart to her scullionhood, and it has taken her into the high-instep circle. I read the other day of his daughter's marriage to some English nob, and of the discovery of the ancient Reinhart family tree and crest with the mailed hand and two-edged dirk and the vulture rampant, and the motto, 'Who strikes in the back strikes often.'"

He left me with his laugh still ringing in my ears. I shuddered as I passed under the old black-and-gold sign my uncle and my father had nailed over the office entrance in an age now dead, an age when Wall Street men talked of honour and gold, not gold and more gold.

In telling my wife of the day's happenings I could not refrain from giving vent to the feelings that consumed me. "Kate, Bob will surely do something awful one of these days. I can see no hope for him. He grows more and more the madman as he broods over his horrible situation. The whole thing seems incredible to me. Never was a human being in such perpetual living purgatory—unlimited, absolute power on the one hand, unfathomable, never-cool-down hell on the other."

"Jim, how does he do what he does? I cannot make out from anything I have read or you have told me, how he creates those panics and makes all that money."

"No one has ever been able to figure it out," I answered. "I understand the stock business, but I cannot for the life of me see how he does it. He has none of the money powers in league with him, that's sure, for in the mood he has been in during the past two years it would be impossible for him to work with them, even if his salvation depended on it. The mention of any of the big 'System' men drives him to a fury. He has to-day made more money than any one man ever made in a day since the world began, and he had only commenced his work when he quit to please me. As I stand in the Exchange and watch him do it, it seems commonplace and simple. Afterward it is beyond my comprehension. At the gait he is going, the Rockefeller, Vanderbilt, and Gould fortunes combined will look tiny in comparison with the one he will have in a few years. It is beyond my power of figuring out, and it gives me a headache every time I try to see through it."

Chapter VIII

A NUMBER OF times during the following year, and finally on the anniversary of the Sands tragedy, Bob carried the Exchange to the verge of panic, only to turn the market and save "the Street" in the end. His profits were fabulous. Already his fortune was estimated to be between two and three hundred millions, one of the largest in the world. His name had become one of terror wherever stocks were dealt in. Wall Street had come to regard his every deal, from the moment that he began operations, as inevitably successful. Now and again he would jump into the market when some of the plunging cliques had a bear raid under way, and would put them to rout by buying everything in sight and bidding up prices until it looked as though he intended to do as extraordinary work on the up-side as he was wont to do on the down. At such times he was the idol of the Exchange, which worships the man who puts prices up as it hates him who pulls them down. Once when war news flashed over the wires from Washington and rumour had the Cabinet members, Senators, and Congressmen selling the market short on advance information, when the "Standard Oil" banks had put up money rates to 150 per cent, and a crash seemed inevitable, Bob suddenly smashed the loan market by offering to lend one hundred millions at four per cent.; and by buying and bidding up prices at the same time, he put the whole Washington crowd and its New York accomplices to disastrous rout and caused them to lose millions. He continued his operations with increasing violence and increasing profits up to the fourth anniversary of the tragedy. On the intervening anniversary I had been compelled by self-interest and fear that he would really pull down the entire Wall Street structure, to rush in and fairly drag him off. But with his growing madness my influence was waning. Each raid it was with greater difficulty that I got his ear.

Finally, on the fourth anniversary, in a panic that seemed to be running into something more terrible than any previous, he savagely refused to accede to my appeal, telling me that he would not stop, even if Randolph & Randolph were doomed to go down in the crash. It had become known on the floor that I was the only one who could do anything with him in his frenzies, and my pleading with him in the lobby was watched by the members of the Exchange with triple eyed suspense. When it was clear from his emphatic gestures and raised voice—for he was in a reckless mood from drink and madness and took no pains to disguise his intentions—that I could not prevail upon him, there was a frantic rush for the poles to throw over stocks in advance of him. Suddenly, after I had turned from him in despair, there flashed into my mind an idea. The situation was desperate. I was dealing with a madman, and I decided that I was justified in making this last try. I rushed back to him. "Bob, good-bye," I whispered in his ear, "good-bye. In ten minutes you will get word that Jim Randolph has cut his throat!" He stopped as though I had plunged a knife into him, struck his forehead a resounding blow, and into his wild brown eyes came a sickening look of fear.

"Stop, Jim, for God's sake, don't say that to me. My cup is full now. Don't tell me I am to have that crime on my soul." He thought a moment. "I don't know whether you mean it, Jim, but I can take no chances, not for all the money in the world, not even for revenge. Wait here, Jim." He yelled for his brokers, and several rushed to him from different parts of the room. He sent them back into the crowd while he dashed for the Amalgamated-pole. The day was saved.

Presently he came back to me. "Jim, I must have a talk with you. Come over to my office." When we got there he turned the key and stood in front of me. His great eyes looked full into mine. In college days, gazing into their brown depths, by some magic I seemed to see the heroes and heroines of always happy-ending tales, as the child sees enchanted creatures far back in the burning Yule log flames. But there were no joyous beings in the haunted depths of Bob's eyes that day.

"Jim, you gave me an awful scare," he said brokenly. "Don't ever do it again. I have little left to live for. To be sure I have some feeling for mother, Fred, and sisters. But for you I have a love second only to that I should have felt for Beulah had I been allowed to have her. The thought, Jim, that I had wrecked your life, with all you have to live for, would have been the last straw. My life is purgatory. Beulah is only an ever-present curse to me—a ghost that rends my heart and soul, one minute with a blind frenzy to revenge her wrongs, the next with an icy remorse that I have not already done so. If I did not have her, perhaps in time I could forget; perhaps I might lay out some scheme to help poor devils whose poverty makes life unendurable, and with the millions I have taken from that main shaft of hell I might do things that would at least bring quiet to my soul; but it is impossible with the living corpse of Beulah Sands before me every minute and that devil machinery whirling in my brain all the time the song, 'Revenge her and her father, revenge yourself.' It is impossible to give it up, Jim. I must have revenge. I must stop this machinery that is smashing up more American hearts and souls each year than all the rest of earth's grinders combined. Every day I delay I become more fiendish in my desires. Jim, don't think I do not know that I have literally turned into a fiend. Whenever of late I see myself in the mirror, I shudder. When I think of what I was when your father stood us up in his office and started us in this heart-shrivelling, soul-callousing business, and what I am now, I cannot keep the madness down except with rum. You know what it means for me to say this, me who started with all the pride of a Brownley; but it is so, Jim. The other night I went home with my soul frozen with thoughts of the past and with my brain ablaze with rum, intending to end it all. I got out my revolver, and woke Beulah, but as I said, 'Bob is going to kill Beulah and himself,' she laughed that sweet child's laugh and clapping her hands said, 'Bob is so good to play with Beulah,' and then I thought of that devil Reinhart and the other fiends of the 'System' being left to continue their work unhindered and I could not do it. I must have revenge; I must smash that heart-crushing machinery. Then I can go, and take Beulah with me. Now, Jim, let us have it clearly understood once and for all."

Remorse and softness were past; he was the Indian again. "I am going to wreck that hell-annex some day, and that some day will be the next time I start in. Don't argue with me, don't misunderstand me. To-day you stopped me. I don't know whether you meant what you threatened; I don't care now. It is just as well that I stopped, for the 'System's' machine will be there whenever I start in again. It loses nothing of its fiendishness, none of its destructive powers by grinding, but, on the contrary, as you know, it increases its speed every day it runs. Now, Jim Randolph, I want to tell you that you must get yours and the house's affairs in such shape that you won't be hurt when I go into that human rat-pit the next time, for when I come from it the New York Stock Exchange and the 'System' will have had their spines unjointed. Yes, and I'll have their hearts out, too. Neither will ever again be able to take from the American people their savings and their manhood and womanhood and give them in exchange unadulterated torment. I am going to be fair with you, Jim; this is the last time I will discuss the subject. After this you must take your chance with the rest of those who have to do with the cursed business. When I strike again, none will be spared. I will wreck 'the Street', and the innocent will go down with the guilty, if they have any stocks on hand at that time.

"My power, Jim, is unlimited; nothing can stay it. I am not going to explain any further. You have seen me work. You must know that my power is greater than the 'System's,' and you and I and 'the Street' have always known that the 'System' is more powerful than the Government, more powerful than are the courts, legislatures, Congress, and the President of the United States combined, that it absolutely controls the foundation on which they rest—the money of the nation. But my power is greater, a thousand, yes, a million times greater than theirs. Jim, they say that I have made more money than any man in the world. They say that I have five hundred millions of dollars, but the fools don't keep track of my movements. They only know that I have pulled five hundred millions from my open whirls, the ones they have had an opportunity to keep tab on. But I tell you that I have made even more in my secret deals than the amount they have seen me take. I have had my agents with my capital in every deal, every steal the 'System' has rigged up. The world has been throwing up its hands in horror because Carnegie, the blacksmith of Pittsburgh, pulled off three hundred millions of swag in the Steel hold-up—yes, swag, Jim. Don't scowl as though you wanted to read me a lecture on the coarseness of my language. I have learned to call this game of ours by its right name. It is not business enterprise with earned profits as results, but pulled-off tricks with bags of loot—black-jack swag—for their end.

"I got away with three hundred millions when Steel slumped from 105 to 50 and from 50 to 8, and no one knew I'd made a dollar. You and 'the Street' read every morning last year the 'guesses' as to who could be rounding up the hundreds of millions on the slump. The papers and the market letters one morning said it was 'Standard Oil'; the next, that it was Morgan; then it was Frick, Schwab, Gates, and so on down through the list. Of course, none of them denied; it is capital to all these knights of the road to be making millions in the minds of the world, even though they never get any of the money. Dick Turpin and Jonathan Wild never were fonder of having the daring hold-ups that other highwaymen perpetrated laid to their doors, than are these modern bandits of being credited with ruthless deeds that they did not commit. But Jim, 'twas I, 'twas I who sold Pennsylvania every morning for a year, while the selling was explained by the press as 'Cassatt cutting down Gould's telegraph poles. Gould and old man Rockefeller selling Pennsylvania to get even.' Jim Randolph, I have to-day a billion dollars, not the Rockefeller or Carnegie kind, but a real billion. If I had no other power but the power to call to-morrow for that billion in cash, it would be sufficient to lay in waste the financial world before to-morrow night. You are welcome, Jim, to any part of that billion, and the more you take the happier you will make me, but when I strike in again, don't attempt to stay me, for it will do no good."

Shortly after this talk Bob left for Europe with Beulah. A great German expert on brain disorders had held out hope that a six month's treatment at his sanitarium in Berlin might aid in restoring her mind. They returned the following August. The trip had been fruitless. It was plain to me that Bob was the same hopelessly desperate man as when he left, more hopeless, more desperate if anything than when he warned me of his determination.

When he left for Europe "the Street" breathed more freely, and as time went by and there was no sign of his confidence-disturbing influence in the market, the "System" began to bring out its deferred deals. Times were ripe for setting up the most wildly inflated stock lamb-shearing traps. It had been advertised throughout the world that Tom Reinhart, now a two-hundred-time millionaire, was to consolidate his and many other enterprises into one gigantic trust with twelve billions of capital. His Union and Southern Pacific Railroads, his coal and Southern lines, together with his steamship company and lead, iron, and copper mines, were to be merged with the steel, traction, gas, and other enterprises he owned jointly with "Standard Oil." Some of the railroads owned by Rockefeller and his pals, in which Reinhart had no part, were to go in too, and with these was to unite that mother hog of them all, "Standard Oil" itself. The trust was to be an enormous holding company, the like of which had until then not even been dreamed of by the most daring stock manipulators. The "System's" banks, as well as trust and insurance companies throughout the country, had for a long time been getting into shape by concentrating the money of the country for this monster trust. It was newspaper and news bureau gossip that Reinhart and his crowd had bought millions of shares of the different stocks involved in the deal, and it was common knowledge that upon its successful completion Reinhart's fortune would be in the neighbourhood of a billion. On October 1st the certificate of the Anti-People's Trust, $12,000,000,000 capital, 120,000,000 shares, were listed upon the New York, London, and Boston Stock Exchanges, and the German and French Bourses, and trading in them started off fast and furious at 106. The claim that one billion of the twelve billions capital had been set aside to be used in protecting and manipulating the stock in the market, had been so widely advertised that even the most daring plunger did not think of selling it short.

It was evident to all in the stock-gambling world that this was to be the "System's" grand coup, that at its completion the masses would be rudely awakened to a realisation that their savings were invested in the combined American industries at vastly inflated values, that the few had all the real money, and that any attempt upon the people's part to regulate and control the new system of robbery, would be fraught with unparalleled disaster—not to the "System," but to the people.

Since Bob's return from Europe I had seen him but a few times. Up to October 1st he had not been near the Stock Exchange or "the Street." Shortly after the listing of the "People Be Damned," as "the Street" had dubbed the new trust, he began to show up at his office regularly. This was the condition of affairs when Fred Brownley called me up on the telephone, as I related at the beginning of my story, which I did not realise I had been so long in telling.

My thoughts had been chasing each other with lightning-like rapidity back over the last five years and the fifteen before them, and each thought deepened the black mist over my present mental vision. In the midst of my reflections my telephone rang again.

"Mr. Randolph, for Heaven's sake have you done nothing yet?" It was Fred Brownley's voice. "Things are frightful here. Bob's brokers are selling stocks at five and ten thousand-lot clips. Barry Conant is leading Reinhart's forces. It is said he has the pool's protection order in Anti-People's and that it is unlimited, but Bob has the Reinhart crowd pretty badly scared. Swan has just finished giving Conant a hundred thousand off the reel in 10,000 lots, and he told me a moment ago he was going over to get Bob himself to face Barry Conant. They're down twenty points on the average, although they haven't let Anti-People's break an eighth yet. They have it pegged at 106, but there is an ugly rumour just in that Bob, under cover of a general attack, is unloading Anti-People's on to the Reinhart wing for Rogers and Rockefeller, and the rumour is getting in its work. Even Barry Conant is growing a bit anxious. The latest talk is that Reinhart is borrowing hundreds of millions on Anti-People's, and that his loans are being called in all directions. Do you know Reinhart is at his place in Virginia and cannot get here before to-morrow night? If Bob breaks through Anti-People's peg, it will be the worst crash yet."

"All right, Fred," I answered. "I will go over to Bob's right now. I hate to do it, but there is no other hope."

I dropped the receiver and started for Bob's office. As I went through his counting-room one of the clerks said, "They have just broken Anti-People's to 90 on a bulletin that Tom Reinhart's wife and only daughter have been killed in an automobile accident at their place in Virginia. They first had it that Reinhart himself was killed. That has been corrected, although the latest word is that he is prostrated."

I rapped on Bob's private-office door. I felt the coming struggle as I heard his hoarse bellow, "Come in." He stood at the ticker, with the tape in one hand, while with the other he held the telephone receiver to his ear. My God, what a picture for a stage! His magnificent form was erect, his feet were as firmly planted as if he were made of bronze, his shoulders thrown back as if he were withstanding the rush of the Stock Exchange hordes, his eyes afire with a sullen, smouldering blaze, his jaw was set in a way that brought into terrible relief the new, hard lines of desperation that had recently come into his face. His great chest was rising and falling as though he were engaged in a physical struggle; his perfect-fitting, heavy black Melton cutaway coat, thrown back from the chest, and a low, turned-down, white collar formed the setting for a throat and head that reminded one of a forest monarch at bay on the mountain crag awaiting the coming of the hounds and hunters.

I hesitated at the threshold to catch my breath, as I took in the terrific figure. Had Bob Brownley been an enemy of mine I should have backed out in fear, and I do not confess to more than my fair share of cowardice. Inwardly I thanked God that Bob was in his office instead of on the floor of the Exchange. His whole appearance was frightful. He showed in every line and lineament that he was a man who would hesitate at nothing, even at killing, if he should find a human obstacle in his road and his mind should suggest murder. He was the personification of the most awful madness. Even when he caught sight of me, he hardly moved, although my coming must have been a surprise.

"So it is you, Jim Randolph, is it? What brings *you* here?" His voice was hoarse, but it had a metallic ring that went to my marrow. Bob Brownley in all the years of our friendship had never spoken to me except in kind and loving regard. I looked at him, stunned. I must have shown how hurt I was. But if he saw it, he gave no sign. His eyes, looking straight into mine, changed no more than if he had been addressing his deadliest enemy.

Again his voice rang out, "What brings you here? Do you come to plead again for that dastard Reinhart after the warning I gave you?"

I clenched both hands until I felt the nails cut the flesh of my palms. I loved Bob Brownley. I would have done anything to make him happy, would willingly have sacrificed my own life to protect his from himself or others, but this madman, this wild brute, was no more Bob Brownley as I had known him than the howling northeast gale of December is the gentle, welcome zephyr of August; and I felt a resentment at his brutal speech that I could hardly suppress. With a mighty effort I crushed it back, trying to think of nothing but his awful misery and the Bob of our college days.

I said in a firm voice, "Bob, is this the way to talk to me in your own office?" At any time before, my words and tone would have touched his all-generous Southern chivalry, but now he said harshly—"To hell with sentiment. What——" He did not take his eyes from mine, but they told me that he was listening to a voice in the receiver. Only for a second; then he let loose a wild laugh, which must have penetrated to the outer office.

"Eighty and coming like a spring freshet," he said into the mouthpiece, "and the boys want to know if I won't let up now that Reinhart is down? Go back and smother them with all they will take down to 60. That's my answer. Tell them if Reinhart had ten more wives and daughters and they were all killed, I'd rend his bastard trust to help him dull his sorrow. Give the word at every pole that I will have Reinhart where he will curse his luck that he was not in the automobile with the rest of his tribe——

"To hell with sentiment!" He was speaking to me again. "What do you want? If you are here to beg for Reinhart and his pack of yellow curs, you've got your answer. I wouldn't let up on that fiendish hyena, not if his wife and daughter and all the dead wives and daughters of every 'System' man came back in their grave clothes and begged. I wouldn't let up a share." I gasped in horror.

FRIDAY, THE THIRTEENTH

"When did those robbers of men and despoilers of women and children ever let up because of death? When were they ever known to wait even till the corpse stiffened to pluck out the hearts of the victims? It is my turn now, and if I let up a hair may I, yes, and Beulah, too, be damned, eternally damned."

I could not stand it. If I stayed, I, too, should become mad. I reached for the doorknob, but before I could swing the door open Bob was upon me like a wolf. He grasped me by the shoulders and with the strength of a madman hurled me half across the room. I sank into a chair.

"No, you don't, Jim Randolph, no, you don't. You came here for something and, by heaven, you will tell me what it is! You know me; you are the only human being who does. You know what I was, you see what I am. You know what they did to me to make me what I am. You know, Jim Randolph, you know whether I deserved it. You know whether in all my life up to the day those dollar-frenzied hounds tore my soul, I had done any man, woman, or child a wrong. You know whether I had, and now you are going to sneak off and leave me as though I were a cur dog of the Reinhart-'Standard Oil' breed gone mad!"

He was standing over me, a terrible yet a magnificent figure. As he hurled these words at me, I was sure he had really lost his mind; that I was in the presence of a man truly mad. But only for an instant; then my horror, my anger turned to a great, crushing, all-consuming agony of pity for Bob, and I dropped my head on my hands and wept. It is hard to admit it, but it is true—I wept uncontrollably. In an instant the room was quiet except for the sound of my own awful grief. I heard it, was ashamed of it, but I could not stop. The telephone rang again and again, wildly, shrilly, but there was no answer. The stillness became so oppressive that even my own sobs quieted. I gasped as the lump in my throat choked me, then I slowly raised my eyes.

Bob's towering figure was in front of me. His head had fallen forward, and his arms were folded across his breast. But that he stood erect I should have thought him dead, so still was he. I jumped to my feet and looked into his face, down which great tears were dropping silently. I touched him on the shoulder.

"Bob, my dear old chum, Bob, forgive me. For God's sake, forgive me for intruding on your misery."

I looked at him. I will never forget his face. No heartbroken woman's could have been sadder. He slowly raised his head, then staggered and grasped the ticker-stand for support.

"Don't, Jim, don't—don't ask me to forgive you. Oh, Jim, Jim, my old friend, forgive me for my madness; forget what I said to you, forget the brute you just saw and think of me as of old, when I would have plucked out my tongue if I had caught it saying a harsh word to the best and truest friend man ever had. Jim, forget it all. I was mad, I am mad, I have been mad for a long time, but it cannot last much longer. I know it can't, and, Jim, by all our past love, by the memories of the dear old days at St. Paul's and at Harvard, the dear old days of hope and happiness, when we planned for the future, try to think of me only as you knew me then, as you know that I should now be, but for the 'System's' curse."

The clerks were pounding on the door; through the glass showed many forms. They had been gathering for minutes while Bob talked in his low, sad tone, a tone that no one could believe came from the same mouth that a few moments before had poured forth a flood of brutal heartlessness.

Bob went to the door. The office was in an uproar. Twenty or thirty of Bob's brokers were there, aghast at not getting a reply to their calls. Many more were pouring in through the outer office. Bob looked at them coldly. "Well, what is the trouble? Is it possible we are down to a point where the Stock Exchange rushes over to a man's office when his wire happens to break down?"

They saw his bluff. You cannot deceive Stock Exchange men, at least not the kind that Bob Brownley employed on panic days, but his coolness reassured them, and when they saw me it was odds-on that they guessed to a man why Bob had ignored his wires—guessed that I had been pleading for the life of "the Street."

"Well, where do you stand?"

Frank Swan answered for the crowd: "The panic is in full swing. She's a cellar-to-ridge-pole ripper. They're down 40 or over on an average. Anti-People's is down to 35, and still coming like sawdust over a broken dam. Barry Conant's house and a dozen other of Reinhart's have gone under. His banks and trust companies are going every minute. The whole Street will be overboard before the close. The governing committee has just called a meeting to see whether it will not be best to adjourn the Exchange over to-day and to-morrow."

Bob listened as if he had been a master at the wheel in a gale, receiving reports from his mates.

There was no trace now of the scene he had just been through. He was cool, masterful, like the seasoned sea-dog who knows that in spite of the ocean's rage and the wind's howl, the wheel will answer his hand and the craft its rudder. "Jim, come over to the Exchange." The crowd followed along. "We have but a minute and I want to have you say you forgive me," he said to me. "I know, Jim, you understand it all, but I must tell you how sorrowful I am that in my madness I should have so forgotten my admiration, respect, and love for you, yes, and my gratitude to you, as to say what I did. I'll do the only thing I can to atone. I will stop this panic and undo as much as possible of my work;

and now that I have wrecked Reinhart I am through with this game forever, yes, through forever."

He pressed my hand in his strong, honest one and strode into the Exchange ahead of the crowd. All was chaos, although the trading had toned down to a sullen desperation. So many houses, banks, and trust companies had failed that no man knew whether the member he had traded with early in the day would on the morrow be solvent enough to carry out his trades. The man who had been "long" in the morning, and had sold out before the crash, and who thought he now had no interest in the panic, found himself with his stock again on hand, because of the failure of the one to whom he had sold, and the price cut in two. The man who was "short" and who a few minutes before had been eagerly counting his profits now knew that they had been turned to loss, because the man from whom he had borrowed his short stocks for delivery would be in no condition to repay for them, the next day, when they should be returned to him. The "short" man was himself, therefore, "long" stocks he had bought to cover his "short" sale. In depressing the price he had been working against his own pocket instead of against the bulls he had thought he was opposing. All was confusion and black despair. There is, indeed, no blacker place than the floor of the Stock Exchange after a panic cyclone has swept it, and is yet lingering in its corners, while the survivors of its fury do not know whether or not it will again gather force.

Chapter IX

THE GOVERNING COMMITTEE was holding a meeting in its room. Bob rushed in unceremoniously.

"One word, gentlemen," he called. "I have more trades outstanding, both buys and sells, than any other member or house. Before deciding whether to adjourn in an attempt to save 'the Street', I ask your consideration of this proposition: If the Exchange will suspend operations for thirty minutes, and allow me to address the members on the floor, I will agree to buy stocks all around the room, until they have regained at least half their drop—all of it, if possible. I will buy until I have exhausted to the last hundred my fortune of a billion dollars. This should make an adjournment unnecessary. I know that this is a most extraordinary request, but you are confronted with a most extraordinary situation, the most remarkable in the history of the Stock Exchange. Already, if what they say on the floor is correct, over two hundred banks and trust companies throughout the country have gone under, and new failures are being announced every minute. Half the members of this and the Boston and Philadelphia Exchanges are insolvent and have closed their doors, or will close them before three o'clock, and the shrinkage in values so far reported runs over fifteen billions. Unless something is done before the close, there will be a similar panic in every Exchange and Bourse in Europe to-morrow."

The committee instantly voted to lay the proposition before the full board. In another minute the president's gavel sounded, and the floor was still as a tomb. All eyes were fixed on the president. Every man in that great throng knew that upon the announcement they were about to hear, might depend, at least temporarily, the welfare, not only of Wall Street, but of the nation, perhaps even of the civilised world. The president spoke:

"Members of the New York Stock Exchange:

"The Governing Committee instructs me to say that Mr. Robert Brownley has asked that operations be suspended for thirty minutes, in order that he be allowed to address you. Mr. Brownley has agreed, if this request be granted, he will upon resumption of operations purchase a sufficient amount of stock to raise the average price of all active shares at least one-half their total drop—all of it, if possible. He agrees to buy to the limit of his fortune of a billion dollars. I now put Mr. Brownley's request to a vote. All those in favour of granting it will signify the same by saying 'Yes.'"

A mighty roof-lifting "Yes" sounded through the room.

"All those opposed, 'No.'"

There was a deathly hush.

"Mr. Brownley will please speak from this platform, and remember, in thirty minutes to the second, I will sound the gavel for the resumption of business."

Bob Brownley strode to the place just vacated by the president. The crowd was growing larger every minute. The ticker was already hissing a tape biograph of this extraordinary situation in brokerage shops, hotels, and banks throughout the country, and in a few minutes the news of it would be in the capitals of Europe. Never before in history did man have such an audience—the whole civilised world. Already arose from Wall, Broad, and New Streets, which surround the Exchange, the hoarse bellow of the gathering hordes. Before the ticker should announce the resumption of business these would number hundreds of thousands, for the financial district for more than an hour had been a surging mob.

FRIDAY, THE THIRTEENTH

For once at least the much-abused phrase, "He looked the part," could be used in all truthfulness. As Robert Brownley threw back his head and shoulders and faced that crowd of men, some of whom he had hurt, many of whom he had beggared, and all of whom he had tortured, he presented a picture such as a royal lion recently from the jungles and just freed from his cage might have made. Defiance, deference, contempt, and pity all blended in his mien, but over all was an I-am-the-one-you-are-the-many atmosphere of confidence that turned my spinal column into a mercury tube. He began to speak:

"Men of Wall Street:

"You have just witnessed a record-breaking slaughter. I have asked permission to talk to you for the purpose of showing you how any member of a great Stock Exchange may at any time do what I have done to-day. Weigh well what I am about to say to you. During the last quarter of a century there has grown up in this free and fair land of ours a system by which the few take from the many the results of their labours. The men who take have no more license, from God or man, to take, than have those from whom they filch. They are not endowed by God with superior wisdom, nor have they performed for their fellow-men any labour or given to them anything of value that entitles them to what they take. Their only license to plunder is their knowledge of the system of trickery and fraud that they themselves have created. No man can gainsay this, for on every side is the evidence. Men come into Wall Street at sunrise without dollars; before that same sun sets they depart with millions. So all-powerful has grown the system of oppression that single men take in a single lifetime all the savings of a million of their fellows. To-day the people, eighty millions strong, are slaving for the few, and their pay is their board and keep. I saw this robbery. I felt the robbers' scourge. I sought the secret. I found it here, here in this gambling-hell. I found that the stocks we bought and sold were mere gambling chips; that the man who had the biggest

125

stack could beat his opponent off the board; that his opponent was the world, because all men directly or indirectly played the stock-gambling game. To win, it was but necessary to have unlimited chips. If chips were bought and sold, on equal terms, by all, no one could buy more than he could pay for, and the game, although still a gambling one, would be fair. A few master tricksters, dollar magicians, long ago seeing this condition, invented the system by which the people are ruthlessly plundered. The system they invented was simple, so simple that for a quarter of a century it has remained undiscovered by the world at large—and even by you, who profess to be experts. No man thought that a free people who had intended to allow all the equal use of every avenue for the attainment of wealth, and who intended to provide for the safeguarding of wealth after it was secured, could be such dolts as to allow themselves to be robbed of all their accumulated wealth by a device as simple as that by which children play at blindman's buff. The process was no more complex than that employed by the robber of old, who took the pebbles from the beach, marked them money, and with the money bought the labour of his fellows, and by the manipulation of that labour and by turning pebbles into money he took away from the labourer the money which he had paid them for the labour until all in the land were slaves of the moneymaker. These few tricksters said: We will arbitrarily manufacture these chips—stocks. After we have manufactured them, we will sell the world what the world can pay for, and then by the use of the unlimited supply we still have we will win away from the world what it has bought, and repeat the operation, until we have all the wealth, and the people are enslaved. To do this there was one thing besides the manufacturing of the chips—stocks—that was absolutely necessary—a gambling-hell, the working of whose machinery would place a selling value upon such chips; a hell where, after selling the chips, they could be won back. I saw that if these tricksters were to be routed and their 'System' was to be destroyed, it must be through the machinery of this Stock Exchange. I studied the machinery, and presently I marvelled that men could for so long have been asses.

"From the very nature of stock-gambling it is necessary, absolutely necessary, that it be conducted under certain rules, unchangeable, unbreakable rules, to attempt to change or break which would destroy stock-gambling. The foundation rule, the rule absolutely necessary for the existence of stock-gambling is: Any member of the Stock Exchange can buy, or sell, between the opening and the closing of the Exchange as many shares of stock as he cares to. With this rule in force his buying and selling cannot be restricted to the amount he can take and pay for, or deliver and receive pay for, because there is not money enough in the world to pay for what under this same rule can be bought and sold in a single session. This is because there have been arbitrarily created by these few tricksters many times more stocks than there is money in existence. The amount of stock that any man can sell in one session of the Exchange is limited only by the amount that he can offer for sale, and he can offer any amount his tongue can utter; and he is not compelled and cannot be compelled to show his ability to deliver what he has offered for sale until after he has finished selling, which is the following day. You will ask as I did: Can this be possible? You will find the answer I found. It is so, and must continue to be so, or there will be no stock-gambling. Mark me, for this statement is weighted with the greatest import to you all. A member of this Exchange can sell as many shares of stock at one session as he cares to offer. If any attempt is made at the session he sells at to compel him either before or after he offers to sell to show his ability to deliver, away goes the stock-gambling structure, because from the very nature of the whole structure of stock-gambling the same shares are sold and resold many times in each session and the seller cannot know, much less show, that he can deliver until he first adjusts with the buyer and the buyer cannot adjust until after he has become such by buying. If a rule were made compelling a seller to show his responsibility before selling, every member would have every other member at his mercy and there could be no stock-gambling. When I had worked this out, I saw that while the few tricksters of the 'System' had a perfect device for taking from the people their wealth, I had discovered as perfect a means of taking away from the few the wealth they had secured from the many. With this knowledge came a conviction that my way was as honest as the 'System's,' in fact more honest than theirs. They took from the innocent, I took from the guilty what had already been dishonestly secured. I determined to put my discovery into practice.

"I might never have done so but for that Sugar panic in which I was robbed of millions by the 'System' through Barry Conant. In that panic the 'System,' with its unlimited resources, filched from the people by the arbitrary manufacture of stocks, and by their manipulation did to me what I afterward discovered I could do to them, without any resources other than my right to do business on the floor of this Exchange. You saw the outcome, in the second Sugar panic, of my first experiment. In a few minutes I cleared a profit of ten million dollars. I could have made it fifty millions, or one hundred and fifty, but I was not then on familiar terms with my new robber-robbing device, and I had yet a heart. To make this ten millions of money, all that was necessary for me to do was to sell more Sugar than Barry Conant could buy. This was easy, because Barry Conant, not knowing of my newly invented trick, could buy only what he could pay for on the morrow, or, at least, what he believed his clients could pay for; while I, not intending to deliver what I sold—unless by smashing the price to a point where I could compel those who had bought to resell to me at millions less than I sold at—could sell unlimited amounts—literally unlimited amounts. When Barry Conant had bought all that he thought he could pay for, he was obliged to beat a retreat in front of my offerings, and I was able to smash, and smash, until the price was so low that he could not by the use of what he had bought, as collateral, borrow sufficient to pay me for what I had sold him. Then he was compelled to turn about and sell what he had bought from me, and when I had rebought it, for ten millions less than I had sold it for, the trick had been turned. I had sold him 100,000 shares say at 220. He had sold them back to me say at 120, and he stood where he had stood at the beginning. He had none of the 100,000 shares. Both of us stood, so far as stock was concerned, where we had stood at the beginning, but as to profits and losses there was this difference: I had ten millions of dollars profits, while Barry Conant's clients, the 'System,' were ten millions losers—and all by a trick. The trick did not differ in principle from the one in constant practice by the 'System.' When the 'System,' after manufacturing Sugar stock, sell 100,000 shares to the people for $10,000,000, they so manipulate the market by the use of the $10,000,000 that they have taken from the people as to scare them into selling the 100,000 shares back to them for $5,000,000. After they have bought they again manipulate the market until the people buy back for $10,000,000 what they sold for $5,000,000. The 'System' commits no legal crime. I committed no legal crime. I had not even infringed any rule of the Exchange, any more than had the 'System' when they performed their trick. Since my experimental panic I have repeatedly put the trick in operation, and each time I have taken millions, until to-day I have in my control, as absolutely as though I had honestly earned them, as the labourer earns his week's wages, or the farmer the price of his crops, over $1,000,000,000, or sufficient to keep enslaved the rest of their lives a million people.

"What do you intelligent men think of this situation? You know, because you know the stock-gambling game, that the American people, with their boasted brains and courage, come year after year with their bags of gold, the result of their prosperous labours, and dump them, hundreds of millions, into this gambling-inferno of yours. You know that they are fools, these silly millions of people whom you term lambs and suckers. You chuckle as, year after year, having been sent away shorn, they return for new shearing. You marvel that the merchants, manufacturers, miners, lawyers, farmers, who have sufficient intelligence to gather such surplus legitimately, would bring it to our gambling-hell, where upon all sides is plain proof that we who conduct the gambling, and who produce nothing, are obliged to take from those who do produce, hundreds of millions each year for expenses, and hundreds of millions each year for profits—for you know that we have nothing to give them in return for what they bring to us. You know that every dollar of the billions lost in Wall Street means higher prices for steel rails, for lumber and cars, and that this means higher passenger and freight rates to the people. You know that when the manufacturer brings his wealth to Wall Street and is robbed of it, he will add something to the price of boots and shoes, cotton and woollen clothes, and other necessities that he makes and that he sells to the people. You know that when the copper, lead, tin, and iron miners part with their surplus to the 'System,' it means higher prices to the people for their copper pots and gutters, for the water that comes through lead pipes, for their tin dippers and wash boilers, and for their rents, and all those necessities into which machinery, lumber, and other raw and finished material enters. You know that every hundred millions dropped by real producers to the brigands of our world means lower wages or less of the necessities and luxuries for all the people, and especially for the farmer. You know that it is habit with us of Wall Street to gloat over the doctrine of the 'System,' which the people parrot among themselves, the doctrine that the people at large are not affected by our gambling, because they, the people, having no surplus to gamble with, never come into Wall Street. And yet, knowing all this, you never thought, with all your wisdom and cynicism, that right here in this institution, which you own and control, was the open sesame, for each or all of you, to those great chests of gold that your clients, the 'System,' have filled to bursting from the stores of the people. What, I ask, do you wise men think of the situation as you now see it?"

FRIDAY, THE THIRTEENTH

There was an oppressive stillness on the floor. The great crowd, which now contained nearly all the members of the Exchange, listened with bulging eyes and open mouths to the revelations of their fellow member. From time to time, as Bob Brownley poured forth his shot and shell of deadly logic, from the vast mob that now surrounded the Exchange rose a hoarse bellow of impatience, for few in that dense throng outside could understand the silence of the gigantic human crusher, which between the hours of ten and three was never before known to miss a revolution except while its victims' hearts and souls were being removed from its gears and meshes.

Bob Brownley paused and looked down into the faces of the breathless gamblers with a contempt that was superb. He went on:

"Men of Wall Street, it is writ in the books of the ancients that every evil contains within itself a cure or a destroyer. I do not pretend that what I am revealing to you is to you a cure for this hideous evil, but I do say that what I am giving you is a destroyer for it, and that while it will be to the world a cure, it may leave you in a more fiery hell than the one of which you now feel the flames. I do not care if it does. When I am through, any member of the New York Stock Exchange who feels the iron in his soul can get instant revenge and unlimited wealth. You who are turning over in your minds the consideration that your great body can make new rules to render my discovery inoperative, are dealing with a shadow. There is no rule or device that can prevent its working. There are one thousand seats in the New York Stock Exchange. They are worth to-day $95,000 apiece, or $95,000,000 in all. Their value is due to the fact that this Exchange deals in between one and three million shares a day. Were any attempt made to prevent the operation of my invention, transactions would because of such attempt drop to five or ten thousand shares per day, or to such transactions as represent stock that will be actually delivered and actually paid for. To make my invention useless it must be made impossible to buy or sell the same share of stock more than once at one session, and short selling, which is now, as you know, the foundation of the modern stock-gambling structure, must likewise be made impossible. If this could be done the $95,000,000 worth of seats in the Exchange would be worth less than five millions, and, what is of far greater import to all the people, the financial world would be revolutionised. Men of Wall Street, do not fool yourselves. My invention is a sure destroyer of the greatest curse in the world, stock-gambling."

A sullen growl rose from the gamblers. Robert Brownley glared down his defiance.

"Let me show you the impossibility of preventing in the future anyone's doing what I have done to you so many times during the past five years. All the capital required to work my invention is nerve and desperation, or nerve without desperation. It is well known to you that there are at all times Exchange members who will commit any crime, barring perhaps murder, to gain millions. Your members have from time to time shown nerve or desperation enough to embezzle, raise certificates, give bogus checks, counterfeit stocks and bonds, and this for gain of less than millions, and when detection was probable. All these are criminal offences and their detection is sure to bring disgrace and State prison. Yet members of this Exchange desperate enough to take the chance, when confronted with loss of fortune and open bankruptcy, have always been found with nerve enough to attempt the crimes. I repeat that there are at all times Exchange members who will commit any crime, barring perhaps murder, to gain millions. That you may see that my successors will surely come from your midst from time to time during the future existence of the Exchange, I will enumerate the different classes of members who will follow in my footsteps:

"First, the 'In Gold We Trust' schemer who is of the 'System' type, but who is outside the magic circle. A man of this class will reason: I know scores of men, who stand high on 'the Street' and in the social world, who have tens of millions that they have filched by 'System' tricks, if not by legal crimes. If I perform this trick of Brownley's, the trick of selling short until a panic is produced, I shall make millions and none will be the wiser. For all I know, many of the multi-millionaires whom I have seen produce panics and who were applauded by 'the Street' and the press for their ability and daring, and whose standing, business and social, is now the highest, were only doing this same thing, and having been successful, they have never been detected or suspected. But even suppose I fail, which can only be through some extraordinary accident happening while I am engaged in selling, I shall have committed no crime, and, in fact, shall have done no one any great moral wrong, for if I fail to carry out my contract to deliver the stock I have sold in trying to produce a panic, the men to whom I have sold will be no worse off for not receiving what they bought; in fact they will stand just where they stood before I attempted to bring on a panic.

"Second, if an Exchange member for any reason should find himself overboard and should realise that he must publicly become bankrupt and lose all, he surely would be a fool not to attempt to produce a panic, when its production would enable him to recoup his losses and prevent his failure, and when if by accident he should fail in his attempt to produce a panic, the penalty would simply be his bankruptcy, which would have taken place in any event.

"The third class is that large one that always will exist while there is stock-gambling, a class of honest, square-dealing-play-the-game-fair-Exchange men who would take no unfair advantage of their fellow-members until they become awakened to the knowledge that they are about to be ruined by their fellow-members' trickery.

"Next, let us consider further whether it is possible for our Exchange to prevent my device from being worked, now that it is known to all. Suppose the Governing Committee was informed in advance that the attempt to work the trick was to be made. If, at any session, after gong-strike, the Governing Committee, or any Exchange authority, could for any reason compel a member to cease operating, even for the purpose of showing that his transactions were legitimate, the entire structure of stock-gambling would fall. Think it through: Suppose a man like Barry Conant or myself, or any active commission broker, begins the execution of a large order for a client, one, say, who has advance information of a receivership, a fire at a mine, the death of a President, a declaration of war, or any of the hundred and one items of information that must be acted upon instantly, where a delay of a minute would ruin the broker, or his house, or its clients. If the Governing Committee could thus call the broker to account, the professional bear or the schemer, who desired to prevent him from selling, would have but to pass the word to the president of the Exchange that the broker in question was about to work Brownley's discovery and he could be taken from the crowd and before he returned his place could be taken by others and he could be ruined.

"Men of Wall Street, it is impossible to prevent the repetition of those acts by which in five years I have accumulated a billion dollars, impossible so long as a short sale or a repurchase and resale, is allowed. When short sales, and repurchases and resales, are made impossible, stock speculation will be dead. When stock speculation is dead, the people can no longer be robbed by the 'System.' In leaving you, the Exchange, and stock-gambling forever, as I shall when I leave this platform, I will say from the depth of a heart that has been broken, from the profundity of a soul that has been withered by the 'System's' poison, with a full sense of my responsibility to my fellow-man and to my God, that I advise every one of you to do what I have done and to do it quickly, before the doing of it by others shall have made it impossible, before the doing of it by others shall have blown up the whole stock-gambling structure. In accepting my advice you can quiet your conscience, those of you who have any, with this argument: 'If I start, I am sure of success. If I succeed, no one will be the wiser. The millions I secure I will take from men who took them from others, and who would take mine. The more I and others take, the sooner will come the day when the stock-gambling structure will fall.'

"The day on which the stock-gambling structure falls is the day for which all honest men and women should pray."

Bob Brownley paused and let his eyes sweep his dumfounded audience. There was not a murmur. The crowd was speechless.

Again his eyes swept the room. Then he slowly raised his right hand with fist clenched, as though about to deal a blow.

"Men of Wall Street"—his voice was now deep and solemn—"to show that Robert Brownley knew what was fitting for the last day of his career, he has revealed to you the trick—and more.

"Many of you are desperate. Many of you by to-morrow will be ruined. The time of all times for such to put my trick in practice is now. The victim of victims is ready for the experiment. I am he. I have a billion dollars. With this billion dollars I am able to buy ten million shares of the leading stocks and to pay for them, even though after I have bought they fall a hundred dollars a share. Here is your chance to prevent your ruin, your chance to retrieve your fortune, your chance to secure revenge upon me, the one who has robbed you."

He paused only long enough for his astounding advice to connect with his listener's now keenly sensitive nerve centres; then deep and clear rang out, "Barry Conant." The wiry form of Bob's old antagonist leaped to the rostrum.

"I authorise you to buy any part of ten million shares of the leading stocks at any price up to fifty points above the present market. There is my check-book signed in blank, and I authorise you to use it up to a billion dollars, and I agree to have in bank to-morrow sufficient funds to meet any checks you draw. You have failed to-day for seven millions, and, therefore, cannot trade, but I herewith announce that I will pay all the indebtedness of Barry Conant and his house. Therefore he is now in good standing." Bob had kept his eye on the great clock; as the last word passed his lips, the President's gavel descended.

With a mighty rush the gamblers leaped for the different poles. Barry Conant with lightning rapidity gave his orders to twenty of his assistants, who, when Bob Brownley called for Conant, had gathered around their chief. In less than a minute the dollar-battle of the age was on, a battle such as no man had ever seen before. It required no supernatural wisdom for any man on the floor to see that Bob Brownley's seed had fallen in superheated soil, that his until now secret hellite was about to be tested. It needed no expert in the mystic art of deciphering the wall hieroglyphics of Old Hag Fate to see that the hands on the clock of the "System" were approaching twelve. It needed no ear trained to hear human heart and soul beats to detect the approaching sound of onrushing doom to the stock-gambling structure. The deafening roar of the brokers that had broken the stillness following Robert Brownley's fateful speech had awakened echoes that threatened to shake down the Exchange walls. The surging mob on the outside was roaring like a million hungry lions in an Arbestan run at slaughter time.

Chapter X

The instant after the gong sounded Bob Brownley was alone on the floor at the foot of the president's desk. His form was swaying like a reed on the edge of the cyclone's path. I jumped to his side. His brother, who had during Bob's harangue been vainly endeavouring to beat his way through the crowd, was there first. "For God's sake, Bob, hear me. Word came from your house half an hour ago of the miracle: Beulah has awakened to her past. Her mind is clear; the nurses are frantic for you to come to her."

He got no further. With a mad bellow and a bound, like a tortured bull that sees the arena walls go down, Bob rushed out through the nearest door, which, I thanked God, was a side one leading to the street where the crowd was thinnest. He cast a wild look around. His eyes lighted on an empty automobile whose chauffeur had deserted to the crowd. It was the work of a second to crank it; of another to jump into the front seat. Quick as had been his movement, I was behind him in the rear seat. With a bound the great machine leaped through the crowd.

"In the name of Christ, Bob, be careful," I yelled, as he hurled the iron monster through the throng, scattering it to the right and left as the mower scatters the sheaves in the wheat fields. Some were crushed beneath its wheels. Bob Brownley heard not their screams, heard not the curses of those who escaped. He was on his feet, his body crouched low over the steering-wheel, which he grasped in his vise-like hands. His hatless head was thrust far out, as though it strove to get to Beulah Sands ahead of his body. His teeth were set, and as I had jumped into the machine I had noted that his eyes were those of a maniac, who saw sanity just ahead if he could but get to it in time. His ears were deaf not only to the howl of the terrified throng and the curses of the teamsters who frantically pulled their horses to the curb, but to my warnings as well. He swung the machine around the corner at New Street and into Wall as though it had been the broadest boulevard in the park. He took Wall Street at a bound I was sure would land us through the fence into Trinity's churchyard. But no. Again he turned the corner, throwing the Juggernaut on its outside wheels from Wall Street into Broadway as the crowds on the sidewalk held their breath in horror. I, too, was on my feet, but crouching as I hung to the sides. Thank God, that usually crowded thoroughfare was free from vehicles as far up as I could see, on beyond the Astor House. What could it mean? Was that divinity which 'tis said protects the drunkard and the idiot about to aid the mad rush of this love-frenzied creature to his long-lost but newly returned dear one? I heard the frantic clang of gongs, and as we shot by the World Building, I saw ahead of us two plunging automobiles filled with men. 'Twas from them the gong clamour sounded. As we drew nearer. I saw that these were the cars of the fire chiefs answering a call. I thanked God again and again as I yelled into Bob's ear, "For Beulah's sake, Bob, don't pass; if you do, we'll run into a blockade. If we keep in the rear they'll clear our way, and we may get to her alive." I do not know whether he heard, but he held the machine in the rear of the other cars and did not try to pass. Away we went on our mad rush through crowded Broadway. At Union Square we lost our way-clearers. As our automobile jumped across Fourteenth Street into Fourth Avenue, Bob must have opened her up to the last notch, for she seemed to leap through the air. We sent two wagons crashing across the sidewalks into the buildings. Cries of rage arose above the din of the machine, and seemed to follow in our wake. Bob was dead to all we passed. His entire being seemed set on what was ahead. I knew he was an expert in the handling of the automobile, for since his misfortune, automobiling with Beulah Sands had been his favourite pastime, but who could expect to carry that plunging, swaying car to Forty-second Street! Bob seemed to be performing the wondrous task. We shot from curb to curb and around and in front of vehicles and foot passengers as though the driver's eyes and hands were inspired.

Across the square at last and on up Fourth Avenue to Twenty-sixth Street. Then a dizzying whirl into Madison. Was he going to keep to it until he got to Forty-second Street and try to make Fifth Avenue along that congested block with its crush of Grand Central passengers and lines upon lines of hacks and teams? No. His head must be clear. Again he threw the great machine around the corner and into Fortieth Street. For a part of the block our wheels rode the sidewalk, and I awaited the crash. It did not come. Surely the new world Bob was speeding to must be a kind one, else why should Hag Fate, who had been at the steer-wheel of his life-car during the last five years, carry him safely through what looked a dozen sure deaths? Without slacking speed a jot we swung around the corner of Fortieth into Fifth Avenue. The road was clear to Forty-second; there a dense jam of cars, teams, and carriages blocked the crossing. Bob must have seen the solid wall for I heard his low muttered curse. Nothing else to indicate that we were blocked with his goal in sight. He never touched the speed controller, but took the two blocks as though shot from a catapult. The two? No, one, and three-quarters of the next, for when within a score of yards of the black wall he jammed down the brakes, and the iron mass ground and shook as though it would rend itself to atoms, but it stopped with its dasher and front wheels wedged in between a car and a dray. It had not stopped when Bob was off and up the avenue like a hound on the end-in-sight trail. I was after him while the astonished bystanders stared in wonder. As we neared Bob's house I could see people on the stoop. I heard Bob's secretary shout, "Thank God, Mr. Brownley, you have come. She is in the office. I found her there, quiet and recovered. She did not ask a question. She said, 'Tell Mr. Brownley when he comes that I should like to see him.' Then she ordered me to get the afternoon paper. I handed it to her an hour ago. I think she believes herself in her old office. I shut off the floor as you instructed. I did not dare go to her for fear she would ask questions. I have"—but Bob was up the stairs two and three steps at a time.

My breath was almost gone and it took me minutes to get to the second floor. My feet touched the top stair, when, O God! that sound! For five long years I had been trying to get it out of my ears, but now more guttural, more agonised than before, it broke upon my tortured senses. I did not need to seek its direction. With a bound I was at the threshold of Beulah Sands-Brownley's office. In that brief time the groans had stilled. For one instant I closed my eyes, for the very atmosphere of that hall moaned and groaned death. I opened them. Yes, I knew it. There at the desk was the beautiful gray-clad figure of five years ago. There the two arms resting on the desk. There the two beautiful hands holding the open paper, but the eyes, those marvellous gray-blue doors to an immortal soul—they were closed forever. The exquisitely beautiful face was cold and white and peaceful. Beulah Sands was dead. The hell-hounds of the "System" had overtaken its maimed and hunted victim; it had added her beautiful heart to the bags and barrels and hogsheads stored away in its big "business-is-business" safe-deposit vaults. My eyes in sick pity sought the form of my old schoolmate, my college chum, my partner, my friend, the man I loved. He was on his knees. His agonised face was turned to his wife. His clasped hands had been raised in an awful, heart-crushing prayer as his Maker touched the bell. Bob Brownley's great brown eyes were closed, his clasped hands had dropped against his wife's head, and in dropping had unloosed the glorious golden-brown waves until in fond abandon they had coiled around his arms and brow as though she for whom he had sacrificed all was shielding his beloved head from the chills and dark mists of the black river that laps the brink of the eternal rest. The "System" had skewered Robert Brownley's heart too. I staggered to his side. As I touched his now fast-icing brow my eyes fell upon the great black headlines spread across the top of the paper that Beulah Sands had been reading when the all-kind God had cut her bonds:

FRIDAY, THE THIRTEENTH

FRIDAY THE THIRTEENTH

And beneath in one column:

TERRIBLE TRAGEDY IN VIRGINIA

THE RICHEST MAN IN THE STATE, THOMAS REINHART, MULTI-MILLIONAIRE, WHILE TEMPORARILY INSANE FROM THE LOSS OF HIS WIFE AND DAUGHTER, AND OF HIS ENORMOUS FORTUNE, WHICH WAS SHATTERED IN TO-DAY'S AWFUL PANIC, CUT HIS THROAT. HIS DEATH WAS INSTANTANEOUS.

In another column:

ROBERT BROWNLEY CREATES THE MOST AWFUL PANIC IN HISTORY, AND SPREADS WRECK AND RUIN THROUGHOUT THE CIVILISED WORLD.

Publisher's Note

The following are fac-similes of a few of the letters received by the author during the serial publication of "Friday, the Thirteenth."

***

RESIDENCE OF

THE PAULIST FATHERS

2158 PINE STREET

San Francisco, CA

21 October 1906

My Dear Mr. Lawson

Kindly allow one of your countless admirers to express his extreme gratification with the announcement that you will add fiction to your distinguished literary achievements. Your gifts as a writer are so wonderful and fascinating that I look forward eagerly to your work in this new field—and I pray God to prosper you in all good.

Sincerely,

John Marus Haudly

***

70 Kirkland St., Cambridge

Dec. 26, 1906.

Mr. T. W. Lawson,

Boston, Mass.

My Dear Sir: Allow me to congratulate you on your last move and on your story, "Friday, the Thirteenth".

It is the best yet, not merely as a story but as an eye opener. I can begin to see daylight in spots, where it looks like a remedy and a real one. I can't see how you will work it; but I think I do get a hint, and it holds me tightly.

That story ought to be issued in a cheap (25¢) edition in paper, and every man in American ought to read it. The third part is yet to come; but, if I mistake not, it will make us all say "Hurrah!" In this form the facts go home. They were too abstract before. Now they live and palpitate. Sincerely yours,

[Illegible: H. W. Majorson]

**

Dowagiac, Mich., Dec 26, 1906.

Mr. T. Lawson,

Boston, Mass.

Dear Sir—

I have just finished reading your second installment of "Friday the 13th." It is one of the greatest stories I ever read. Your previous articles are good, but this is a wonder. I believe you are sincere and cannot help admiring your wonderful courage + grit in going up against big odds. I have no axe to grind with you, simply think that no matter how big you may be you like to know that what you write is appreciated by the majority of good american citizens. So Here's to you Mr Lawson + I back you to eventually win. Smash 'em good.

Yours Truly

    A. J. Hill.

***

Grinnell, Iowa,

Nov. 3 1906

Thomas Lawson

Boston, Mass.

Dear Sir,

What did "Bob" hear when he picked up the receiver. Impossible to wait one month to find out.

Yours truly,

    A. W. Talbott

***

103 Stedman Street

Brookline Mass.

Dear Mr. Lawson:—

I have hit just read the first instalment of your serial "Friday the 13th."

I was so interested, aroused and stirred, I felt I must express to you some of the appreciation I feel for the work you have done and are doing.

The army of those who suffer is so great the human spoilers so strong; that one's heart goes out in gratitude to a champion who comes around and able willing to do better for the oppressed.

Would it be an intrusion to extend sympathy to one bereft of the beautiful gift of loving companionship? I hope that it is sincerely felt.

Many admire and rejoice in your work—may it go forward bringing the knowledge which is power to ever increasing numbers of American people.

Most Sincerely

Marion E. Major

December 14th, 1906

***

L. GUY DENNETT

ATTORNEY AT LAW

48 TREMONT ST., BOSTON

TELEPHONE CONNECTION

Nov. 21/06

Thomas W. Lawson Esq.

Boston, Mass.

Dear Sir,

I take it for granted that you want to know how the "Public" is going to take to your latest writing "fiction" and how are you to know unless your unknown friends write you?

FRIDAY, THE THIRTEENTH

I have read every thing you have ever written because I believe in you and admire the work you have done and are doing and allow me to say that I finaly believe that you will one day be recognized as one of the greatest story writers of the age. The first section of "Friday the Thirteenth" has convinced me that you will be a sure winner.

Yours very truly,

L. Guy Dennett

***

Angola Tulare Co. Cal.

Dec. 29, 1906

W. T. Lawson,

Dear Sir,

I wanted to thank you for the first number of "Friday the 13th", but did not know your address. "Everybody's" contains some letters written you to Boston so hope this may reach its destination.

I live in the wildest of the wooley west + such a god send as in "Everybody's" (sent me by a sister in Oakland Cal.) + containing the first number of your story, words inadequately suffices. Friday the 13th made an impression on me which I could not easily shake off if I would. I was so sorry it ended where it did that I wanted to cry out + could hardly wait for the Jan. number. Yesterday I bought one in Hanford Cal. rode 30 miles north to get it. I live a mile from the recently filled in basin of old Tulare Lake. The snowfall on the mountains argue that our part of the Wild + Wooley may soon be a fishing station instead of an alfalfa ranch.

Perhaps you don't understand how much your story is appreciated.

You are Bob Brownley, *I know*. Can you really *feel* what you write as you make us do? Your characters appeal to me so that I live with them, every nerve alert to the straining point (but with pleasure). You are certainly the idol of the American people. I've heard you discussed by rich + poor, monopolist + antimonopolist during the publication of "Frenzied Finance" + the worst a monopolist could say was that you were as bad as the Standard Oil, but wanted to get even. "What is that but a virtue," exclaimed I. "Couldn't he have made millions by staying in, but *he* recognized his past failings and exposed ~~them~~ S.O. to uphold a nation. May honor attend him. Isn't that being a man and a gentleman?"

People read "Frenzied Finance" to a man + would loan the magazine one to another so those who felt the 15¢ impossible could get the good of your revelations.

I'm glad you believe in sentiment—the heart-lasting sentiment (instead of dollars and desire) which I feared was becoming a thing of the past; There are still splendid men in America. God bless them.

O happy New Year may the weight of your pen sway millions. Amen.

Respectfully,

Louise D. Tennent

See 14 Kings

Angola P.O. Ca.

***

Spokane, Wash.,

December 28. 1906.

FRIDAY, THE THIRTEENTH

Mr. Thomas W. Lawson,

Boston, Mass.

Dear Sir:

I have lived nine years in Anaconda, Montana, and therefore become somewhat familiar with amalgamated copper, etc. I want to say I have followed your writings with lively interest and have sworn by all the statements you have made. It is, therefore, with the greatest regret that I am compelled to state that my faith in you has been shattered.

When you state in your story of "Friday the 13th" that the heroine walked in to an office in New York in the middle of July with a feather turban on her head I simply cannot swallow it. That a lady of refinement and good taste with $30,000 in the bank, and anxious to make a good appearance, should walk into an office in New York with a winter hat taxes my credulity to the breaking point. However, be that as it may, I want to say that you have made a big fight against great odds and that I admire your pluck and genius, and I hope you will keep right on fighting for the right.

By the way, I might as well admit that it was my wife by the way is a superior woman who called my attention to the turban when I was reading your story aloud to her. I am,

Very truly yours,

John Ortson

***

Ill. Nov. 22nd, 1906

Thos W. Lawson

THOMAS WILLIAM LAWSON

Boston, Mass.

Dear Sir,

It has afforded me great pleasure to just have finished your first installment to "Friday the 13th," as have also your previous writings, from which I learned a great deal,—although from a financial standpoint, following what I thought to be your advice, I am several thousand dollars looser,—and I take this means of contributing my mite of encouragement, firmly believing that your work is doing a great good, and trusting that success on the lines you have mapped out, will be your reward.

Very respectfully, Wm. A. Staney.

(I'm awaiting your next installment)

***

Dear sir:

I have only had the pleasure of meeting you once—in your private car, with Thayer, when you were returning from your western trip—but I hope you will not consider me presuming if I take a moment of your valuable time to thank you for your masterpiece just begun in Everybody's.

Such magic has not flowed from a pen for many a year.

Yours Truly

John O Powers

206 North 34th Street

Philadelphia

FRIDAY, THE THIRTEENTH

***

Des Moines, Iowa, 11/20, 1906

Mr. Thos. Lawson

Boston.

Dear Sir,

I like your story "Friday the Thirteenth." For the information and added knowledge your previous writing has given me I thank you.

—"for the crow that is in him and the spurs that are on him to back up the crow with." You certainly are a game and competant old fighter.

Sincerely, with best wishes

[Illegible signature: A. S. Goodman]

***

St. Paul, Minn.,

November 26, 1906.

Mr. Thomas W. Lawson,

Boston, Mass.

Dear Sir:

I wish to congratulate you on the good story you wrote in Everybody's Magazine this month. It is the beat story I ever read and the best I ever saw published in any magazine.

I am well posted on the "Brokers" business and enjoyed your story very much. I hope you will continue to write them. I know they are taken more from real life than immagination. I am sure they will be appreciated as much as "Frenzied Finance". I have taken the liberty to send a good word to Ridgway's.

With best wishes, I remain

Tours respectfully,

Western Union Telegraph Co.

R.A. Kelly

***

Los Angeles, Calif..

December 11, 1906.

Mr. Thomas W. Lawson,

Boston, Mass.

My dear Sir:

It was indeed a pleasure to read your novel in this month's Everybody's. Being an old trader myself, I have appreciated every word of it and look forward for the continuation with much interest.

I just want to say this too—that anyone who says that you cannot write anything else but "Street" gossip had better cover his "shorts".

Wishing you all kinds of success, and with congratulations on your splendid work, I am

Very sincerely,

Nancy Brown

FRIDAY, THE THIRTEENTH

214 Citizens Nat'l Bank Bldg.

***

Washington, D.C.,

December 1, 1906.

Thos. W. Lawson, Esq.,

Boston, Mass.

Dear Sir:

I have just read with very great pleasure and edification the first installment of your excellent story "Friday the 13th". It is so far a masterpiece.

Congratulating you. I remain

Very truly,

M. H. Ramaze

***

Cleburn, Texas, Dec 3 1906

Mr. Thos. W. Lawson

Boston

Dear Sirs:

I have just your first installment of "Friday 13th." It is OK + if the balance of the story is as good (+ I have no doubts on that score) you are "It" when it comes to writting fiction as well as tricking the Insurance Thief + Standard Oil Grafters.

Wishing you success

I am yours very truly

S. F. Welch

***

Rumford Falls, Maine,

November 20, 1906.

Mr. Tom Lewson,

Boston, Mass.

Dear Sir:

I have read all your writings in Everybody's, including the first installment of your story in the December number, and I must say that I am more than pleased with it. As a writer of fiction you are sure to make another big hit.

Yours truly,

W. I. White.

Thirteen Interesting Facts About Friday the 13th

The following thirteen facts were collected surrounding the prevalence of Friday the 13th as a day that many people are superstitious about

1) The fear of the number 13 is so common that you will regularly notice that many hotels and apartment buildings do not have a thirteenth floor. This is because it was not uncommon for guests to request to NOT stay on that floor.

Floors, instead, go from the 12th floor to the 14th floor. Apparently, not being able to easily do the math in their head puts enough people at ease.

2) Following the same reasoning above, there are some airports that do not have a Gate 13

3) Since you're reading this book you might be interested in the various official phobia names associated with the date Friday the 13th as well as the day Friday or the number 13.

a. Paraskevidekatriaphobia and Friggatriskaidekaphobia are two terms that are used for fear of Friday the 13th. Paraskevi is Greek for Friday and Frigg is the Norse God after whom Friday is named

b. Triskaidekaphobia is fear or avoidance of the number 13.

4) On October 13, 1037, officers of King Philip IV of France raided the homes of thousands of 14th-century Knight Templar Crusades warriors. They were imprisoned on charges of various illegal activities which could not be

proven. But in the process, more than a hundred of them died suffering under terrible torture.

5) American President Franklin D. Roosevelt is said to have regularly avoided travel on the 13th day of any month. He also, allegedly, would never host 13 guests at a meal. President Herbert Hoover was also averse to the number 13.

6) Alfred Hitchcock, the director of many classic thriller and horror films was born on the 13th — Interestingly, a film entitled "Number 13," which was supposed to be Hitchcock's directorial debut never made it past the first few scenes and was shut down due to financial problems.

7) One of the most controversial political leaders of his era, and regularly seen as an enemy to the United States, Fidel Castro was born on Friday the 13th, in August 1926.

8) One of the most commonly shared sources for the fear of the number thirteen usually comes from the thirteenth guest at Jesus' Last Supper. Judas, the thirteen at that fateful meal, is said to have either been the thirteen person to arrive or else the first to leave – either on his way from or on his way to his betrayal of Jesus. The death of Jesus is also said to have happened on a Friday

9) The Romans considered the number 13 unlucky, as they believed that twelve was a number that represented completeness. (Consider the elements of twelve months in a calendar year, the twelve signs of the Zodiac)

10) Fear of Friday the 13th is seen by some business people as serious business (and perhaps lucky for some) According

to the Stress Management Center and Phobia Institute in Asheville, N.C., which, offers therapy to help people overcome their fear of Friday the 13th hundreds of millions of dollars of business are lost due to people's fear of flying or doing the business as usual whenever Friday the 13th comes around.

11) In 2012, there were three Friday the 13ths (Jan 13, April 13 and July 13) All three of those dates feel exactly thirteen weeks apart from one another. The previous time that had happened had been in 1984. (Considering the novel that George Orwell wrote about that year, one might also make a connection with that dystopian vision containing its fair share of bad luck

12) Pop music sensation Taylor Swift, who was born on the 13th and turned 13 years old on Friday the 13th, has regularly played with the number 13. The song "The Lucky One" is the 13th track on her *Red* album, contains a 13 second introduction and the work "lucky" is said 13 times in the song. She considers 13 a lucky number, (her Twitter account is taylorswift13), used to regularly draw the number 13 on her hand with eyeliner before each show, and has claimed that when she is seated in row 13 or row M (the 13th letter) at an award show, she always wins.

13) The classic horror film *Friday the 13th* takes place on June 13, 1958 and June 13, 1980—the latter date being a Friday. This film, the first in a huge franchise, made 39,754,601 dollars on a budget of 550,000 dollars. Victor Miller, one of the main writers for the film, admitted he had been riding off the popularity of the John Carpenter

film, *Halloween*. The movie was mostly filmed at Camp No-Be-Bos-Co in Blairstown, New Jersey, a Boy Scout Camp that originated in 1927 and is still in operation and offers "Crystal Lake" tours (Crystal Lake being the fictional setting for the film)

About Mark Leslie

MARK LESLIE is a writer, editor and bookseller who was born and grew up in Sudbury, Ontario, spent many years in Ottawa, and Hamilton, Ontario and currently lives in Waterloo, Ontario.

A writer of horror, thrillers and true tales of the paranormal, Mark has always been fascinated with ghosts, monsters and eerie tales. He would be the first person to tell you that he is still afraid of the dark and of the monster under his bed.

When he's not writing, Mark attaches "Lefebvre" back onto his name and works in the book industry as a trusted author coach and consultant.

A bookselling veteran for more than twenty-five years, Mark has worked at virtually every type of bookstore, has sat on the Board of Directors for BookNet Canada and also been President of the Canadian Booksellers Association.

The former Director of Self-Publishing and Author Relations at Kobo, Mark and his team launched Kobo Writing Life in July of 2012 and it went on to represent 1 in every 4 or 5 books sold in Kobo's global catalog, a larger percentage of sales than any of the major publishers.

Mark hosts a weekly podcast about writing and publishing called Stark Reflections on Writing & Publishing, which appears at www.starkreflections.ca[1] and he continues to travel to give talks about publishing. He has given talks across Canada and the United States, in London, Paris and Frankfurt on the bookselling, writing and publishing industry.

You can find out more about Mark at www.markleslie.ca[2] or follow him on Twitter @MarkLeslie.

Want to read some great eerie horror tales? Sign up for Mark's Author Newsletter[3] and receive a free eBook (Campus Chills) – which contains modern horror tales all set on university and college campuses.

Thirteen of Mark Leslie's Books

Non-fiction paranormal:

- *Haunted Hamilton: The Ghosts of Dundurn Castle and Other Steeltown Shivers* (2012)
- *Spooky Sudbury: True Tales of the Eerie & Supernatural* (2013) – Co-written with Jenny Jelen
- *Tomes of Terror: Haunted Bookstores and Libraries* (2014)
- *Creepy Capital: Ghost Stories of Ottawa and the National Capital*

1. http://www.starkreflections.ca
2. http://www.markleslie.ca
3. http://eepurl.com/i-4Sj

Region (2016)

- *Haunted Hospitals: Eerie Tales about Hospitals, Sanatoriums and Other Institutions* (2017) – Co-written with Rhonda Parrish

Fiction:

- *One Hand Screaming* (2004)
- *Evasion* (2014)
- *I, Death* (2016)
- *A Canadian Werewolf in New York* (2016)

Editor:

- *Campus Chills* (2009)
- *Tesseracts Sixteen: Parnassus Unbound* (2012)
- *Fiction River 23: Editors' Choice* (2017)
- *Fiction River 25: Feel the Fear* (2017)

Mark Leslie's books on Amazon[4]

Mark Leslie's books on Books2Read[5]

Mark Leslie's books on Kobo[6]

Mark Leslie's books on Goodreads[7]

---

4. https://www.amazon.com/Mark-Leslie/e/B004DAC862

5. https://books2read.com/ap/nE2Wv8/Mark-Leslie

6. https://www.kobo.com/p/markleslie

7. https://www.goodreads.com/author/show/391897.Mark_Leslie

www.ingramcontent.com/pod-product-compliance
Lightning Source LLC
Chambersburg PA
CBHW050949120626
46552CB00001B/462